DOLPHIN ISLAND
Lost at Sea

Read all the books in the *Dolphin Island* series:

1. Shipwreck
2. Lost at Sea
3. Survival
4. Fire!
5. Missing
6. Storm Clouds

Jenny Oldfield

DOLPHIN ISLAND

Lost at Sea

Illustrations by
Daniel Howarth

For lovely Lola, Jude and Evan – three dedicated dolphin fans

HODDER CHILDREN'S BOOKS

First published in Great Britain in 2018 by Hodder and Stoughton

1 3 5 7 9 10 8 6 4 2

A CIP catalogue record for this book is available from the British Library.

ISBN 978 1 444 92828 0

Typeset in ITC Caslon 224

Printed and bound in Great Britain by Clays Ltd, St Ives plc

The paper and board used in this book are made from wood from responsible sources.

Hodder Children's Books
An imprint of Hachette Children's Group
Part of Hodder and Stoughton
Carmelite House
50 Victoria Embankment
London EC4Y 0DZ

An Hachette UK Company
www.hachette.co.uk

www.hachettechildrens.co.uk

Chapter One

Alfie Fisher woke in the middle of the night to hear waves crashing on to the shore. They roared in with a rush and a whoosh, drowning out all other sounds.

He lay in the shelter with his eyes wide open, staring up at the canvas roof, waiting patiently for daylight.

On their sleeping mats beside him, his sisters Fleur and Mia were still fast asleep. His dad, James, shifted in his hammock and groaned. His mum, Katie, snored gently.

Alfie remembered what had woken him. It was a bad dream about sailing a small boat into the eye of a mighty storm. The wind howled, the waves rose higher and broke over the deck. He had to hang on to the guardrail for dear life.

Only, it wasn't just a dream, Alfie realized as he lay

in the dark. It had really happened – the tropical storm eight days earlier, the giant waves that had battered their yacht *Merlin* until she'd hit rocks and he'd been tossed overboard. That's how come he was here now with his family, marooned on Dolphin Island. They'd all had to abandon the boat and make for the shore.

A creature scuttled across the floor – light, dry footsteps belonging to something larger than an insect, smaller than a rat. It came and perched on his chest, staring at him with wide lizard eyes.

Alfie's chest rose and fell with his breaths. 'Hello, George,' he whispered to Fleur's pet gecko.

The gecko shot out his long tongue and caught a mosquito.

Are you really George? Alfie wondered. All geckos looked alike to him – small and green and scaly. George was friendlier than the rest due to the fact that Fleur fed him scraps of fruit.

Minutes ticked by but Alfie didn't want to go back to sleep in case the bad dream returned. Instead he counted the insect-bite bumps on his legs and reached twenty-three. Then he planned his day. He would take a swim before breakfast, when hopefully Pearl and the other young dolphins from what he thought of as the Fisher family's special pod would show up. Afterwards he would go beachcombing in the hope of finding useful debris from *Merlin*.

That would be interesting. Who knew what would wash up on to the shore after yesterday's fresh disaster, when *Merlin* had finally broken up on the rocks and sunk without a trace? Maybe more knives from the galley kitchen – they would always come in handy. Foam cushions and mattresses from the cabins would be good too.

He tried to cheer himself up with ideas about what else he could do to make life easier – more coconut-shell cups to drink out of, a fishing rod and line if he found more of the boat's rigging – but his thoughts kept swinging back to the day before and *Merlin*'s disappearance below the waves. She'd stayed there for a week, half a mile offshore – skewered on two splinters of rock, still with most of their precious possessions on board. They'd even built a raft and paddled out there to rescue parts of the mainsail and whatever else they could salvage. Not any more. Yesterday's storm had seen to that.

'Alfie, are you awake?' Six-year-old Mia opened her eyes to a grey half-light.

'Yes,' he whispered.

'Is it time to get up?'

'No. Shush. You'll wake the others.' Aged eleven, he was used to fending off his younger sister's pesky questions.

'I'm thirsty.'

'Wait here,' he told her. He was nearest to the door – it would be easy for him to creep outside and fetch her some water. 'Mind out, George, I have to move.'

As Alfie sat up, the gecko jumped down then darted across the bamboo cane platform, up on to Fleur's shoulder, where he perched happily.

Alfie crawled out on to the white sand. The sky to the east was turning pink and a sliver of golden sun showed on the horizon. The sea shone silver. In the flickering light of the fire that always burned in the spot where they'd made their camp, Alfie unscrewed the top of a white plastic container and carefully poured water into a coconut-shell cup. Wind blew sharp, gritty sand into his face so that he had to scrunch up his eyes and look through half-closed lids.

'Can you pour a drink for me too?' Waking to find George sitting on her shoulder, Fleur had decided to follow Alfie outside. Now she raised her arms high in the air to yawn and stretch, then gathered her long auburn hair into the nape of her neck. With a twist and a tuck she made an untidy bun. 'While you're doing that, I'll put more wood on the fire.'

Fleur knew that keeping the fire going was the most important job on the island. It was what they cooked on and what they would use as a signal if ever a plane or a boat came near. Smoke from the fire told everyone, *Here we are, the Fisher family, stranded on an uninhabited, unnamed island in the middle of the Torres Strait, north of Australia. We were shipwrecked. S.O.S. Please help.*

So Fleur chose dry logs and pieces of driftwood from the pile they collected every day. She placed them on the hot embers, stacking them into a rough pyramid that would let air underneath and allow the flames to

be fanned back into life. Sparks flew upwards and there was a crackle and a sudden blue and orange flare as the logs caught light. 'Have you seen the dolphins this morning?' she asked Alfie as he handed her a drink.

He wiped grit from his face, rubbed his hands on his T-shirt then peered out to sea. 'I haven't had time to look yet.' He searched now for dolphin activity – the sight of grey dorsal fins cutting through the water or of their sleek, domed heads rising to the surface. Scanning the horizon from the glimmering, golden east to the grey west, he saw no sign. 'No, not yet.'

Fleur pursed her lips then sighed. 'Jazz, where are you?' Her day didn't start right unless she caught a glimpse of her own favourite dolphin – Jazz, the tail-walker and acrobat with his lovely dark eyes and downturned mouth. She needed to see him swim up to the shore and slap his tail flukes against the surface of the water, inviting her to come in and swim.

'They'll be here soon,' Alfie guessed. He too longed for a sight of his own favourite – little Pearl with her smooth grey back and pinkish underbelly, the dolphin who had saved him and guided him to land when he'd been thrown from *Merlin* into the sea. He was about to take Mia her drink when he heard her yell from inside the shelter.

'George, get off me!' She shot through the door with the gecko clinging to the top of her head. 'Get him off me, Fleur. I don't like him on my head!'

'Calm down. He won't hurt you,' Fleur scolded. She held out her hand to George who was happy to step on to it and put an end to his rodeo ride out of the shelter. The slack pouch of skin under his chin ballooned in fright.

'It's weird.' Alfie had gone back to searching the waves – not for their pod of friendly dolphins but for bits of wreckage from their boat. 'I can't get used to not seeing *Merlin* stuck on the rocks.'

Fleur agreed. 'We knew she would never sail again, but I still felt better when we could still see her.'

'She made me think of home.' Mia put it simply, standing with her coconut cup held in two hands, brown legs skinny as a seabird's, her hazel eyes filling with tears.

Home for Mia, Alfie and Fleur was England and a

house by the river, next door to Granddad Tony and Nana Joan. Home for Mia meant taking the bus to school and going to after-school club on a Wednesday, receiving glittery face paints for her birthday.

'Never mind, Mi-mi – we'll get back there soon,' Fleur promised. She tried to sound confident and older than her thirteen years.

Mia's bottom lip quivered. 'How?'

'Someone will see our fire. That's why we keep it lit all the time.'

'Who?'

Fleur gazed out to sea, picturing a ship on the limitless, empty horizon. 'Sailors on an oil-tanker,' she said. 'People on a cruise ship.'

'When?' Mia stuck doggedly to her line of questioning. She needed answers.

'Soon.' They'd come full circle and Fleur glanced at Alfie for help.

But he shook his head and turned away. 'I'm going for a walk,' he told them gruffly, striding out across the cool, untrodden sand.

*

'Ouch!' James Fisher found that his broken ribs hurt worse than ever. It was Day 8 on the island and he could scarcely move. Even getting in and out of his hammock made him cry out with pain.

'Stay where you are,' Katie insisted. The sun's rays were creeping inside the shelter. 'I'll bring you breakfast in bed.'

He lay back and groaned. His forehead felt cold and clammy; his mouth was dry. 'This is driving me nuts.'

'You need to stay here and rest. We can manage.' Practical as ever, Katie made him do as he was told. Inwardly she was worried that the break was worse than they'd thought and that a fever had set in. 'I'll send Fleur and Alfie to collect gulls' eggs. Mia can help me slice up some jackfruit.'

'A feast,' he said with a grin then a fresh grimace. He wasn't used to letting the others do all the work. At home, while Katie went out to college to teach, he stayed at home to mend and build, clean and cook. *Home*, he thought. Would they ever get off this island and make it back to where they belonged? Not for the start of term, he was certain. It was already the end of

August and they had spent over a week on the island with no realistic hope of rescue.

'Sleep,' Katie told him gently. 'It'll do you good.'

She waited until he closed his eyes then she went out to rally the troops.

'Where's Alfie?' she asked when she found Mia and Fleur tending the fire. The sun had risen clear of the horizon, casting long, dark shadows across the beach which was edged by sharp rocks and tall palm trees. A single set of footprints curved down towards the sea.

'He went for a walk,' Mia told her.

'Did he say where?'

'He didn't say anything. He just went.' Fleur glanced in the direction Alfie had taken. 'Maybe he went to look for the dolphins.'

'Not before he collects eggs for breakfast.' Katie was strict about this – jobs first, fun later. She was especially keen on the not-going-off-by-yourself rule. 'Always have someone with you,' she would tell them. 'It's not safe to explore alone.' But this morning Alfie had disobeyed her.

'There he is!' Mia pointed to a figure on the headland

to the east. The sun was behind him so it was hard to make him out, except for his bright red shorts. 'Alfie, Mum says to come back!' she yelled and she began to sprint across the sand.

Alfie looked up from the rock pool where he crouched to watch small white crabs waving their claws and scuttling from rock to rock. A grey gull with a bright orange beak swooped down from the clear sky to pluck a crab from a nearby pool.

'Mum says for you to come back,' Mia repeated breathlessly as she reached the rocks. 'You have to fetch eggs. And you forgot to help me mark the calendar stick.'

Alfie frowned and stayed where he was. Today he didn't feel like climbing the cliff behind the camp to collect eggs, and he couldn't be bothered to mark the calendar. In fact, he didn't want to do anything.

'I'll give you a yellow feather for your hat if you come.' Mia tugged at his arm.

'What yellow feather?' The sun was starting to warm his back as he hunched over the pool. The clear water sparkled.

'The curly-wurly one. It fell down from the trees.'

'A cockatoo crest feather,' he realized. Everything his little sister felt showed on her face – just now a mixture of worry that he would get into trouble and glee that she had something precious to offer him. His own face softened into a smile. 'OK, Mia, if you give me a feather, I'll give you these.' He stood up to dip into his shorts pocket and pull out a handful of tiny cowrie shells. 'Fair exchange?'

'Cool!' Mia's eyes lit up. 'All of them?'

Alfie nodded. 'I'll help you to make another necklace out of them if you like.' He looked up the beach at his mum and Fleur standing in front of the shelter next to the fire. A thin thread of smoke rose above the tops of the palm trees, spiralling upwards until it was swept away by the wind. Behind him, the waves broke on the rocks. 'Race you,' he challenged Mia. He would let her win, of course.

So they jumped from the rocks and sprinted up the beach, buffeted by strong gusts, ready to begin another day.

Chapter Two

'Let's count pelicans.' Mia decided on her game for the morning. She jiggled her new cowrie shells between cupped hands and enjoyed the sound of their light rattle. Later she would take Alfie up on his promise to help her make a necklace.

Alfie stood on a rock staring out to sea. Over a week of living on Dolphin Island dressed only in shorts and T-shirt had lightened the tips of his brown hair and his arms and legs were tanned. The soles of his feet had toughened so that he no longer bothered about the rough rock or the hot sand. So far the morning had gone to his mum's plan. He and Fleur had found gulls' eggs for breakfast then Mia had marked the calendar stick. The sun was high in the sky.

'One – two – three ...' Mia started to count the big,

brownish-grey birds as they came in to land. They had long beaks with saggy pouches underneath – the handy place where they stored their catch. 'Four – five …'

'Six!' Alfie pointed out. A pelican dropped from the sky and plunged underwater, coming up with a mouthful of small silver fish. Their tails flipped this way and that in the bird's strong beak before he gulped and swallowed them whole. 'I wish fishing was that easy for us,' he grumbled.

'Hats!' Fleur announced as she climbed the rock to join Mia and Alfie. She handed them over and made sure they jammed them low on to their heads to protect them from the sun. The hats were roughly made from woven palm leaves bound in place by lianas. Mia's was decorated with an array of bright feathers. 'Any dolphins?' Fleur always asked the same question, hoping that the answer would turn out to be yes.

'Nope,' Alfie said. The sea glittered in the sun. It was a deep blue-green, with small white waves breaking far out. *Come on, Pearl*, he thought. *Where are you?*

'Seven – eight …' Mia continued her count.

'I've had an idea that might help us get off the

island,' Fleur told them after a while. She was the one who enjoyed being here the most and felt the least homesick. There wasn't a moment when she wasn't spotting a new species of butterfly, learning about the habits of tree frogs or just kicking back to chat with George. But even she knew they couldn't stay here for ever.

'How?' Every day Alfie racked his brains for a new plan. They'd already built a raft to row out to *Merlin* and rescue some belongings, and they'd explored the coves to either side of their beach, but there were five people altogether and the raft was too flimsy to carry them all. Plus there was the fire – their main hope of being spotted.

'We could write another message in the sand,' Mia suggested. They'd tried that once before when a small plane had flown close by. Fleur had used a stick to write HELP! in giant letters, but the plane had flown away.

'How does that help right now?' Alfie pointed out that they hadn't seen a plane for days.

'No – that won't do. But listen to this.' Eagerly Fleur

described her plan, turning her back to the sea and staring up at the cliff as she spoke. 'You know that we can see a lot further when we're high up than we can at sea level? Well, how about we make a lookout point on top of the cliff? One person could be up there all the time searching for ships in the distance.'

Alfie quickly got the point. 'Taking it in turns?'

'Right. We could all do it, except for Dad. He'll have to wait until he gets better. We could build a second fire up there.'

'And maybe a platform to stand on.' Alfie loved the idea. It reminded him of boy sailors climbing the mainmast on old sailing ships and perching in the crow's-nest to keep a lookout for pirates. 'Let's do it,' he decided.

'Cool!' With a grin, Mia jumped down from the rocks and set off across the sand, with Alfie hot on her heels. They skirted the side of the camp and nimbly began picking their way up the steep cliff behind.

Fleur paused to explain her plan to Katie.

'That's an excellent idea.' James's muffled voice emerged from the shelter.

'You're meant to be asleep,' Katie scolded him. 'Yes, go ahead,' she said to Fleur. 'I'll stay here and keep your dad company. I might do a spot of fishing if I get the chance.'

With a quick high-five, Fleur left her mum and hurried to catch up with the others. Today there was no time to stop and look at the trumpet-shaped scarlet flowers growing in crevices in the dark rock or at the turquoise dazzle of delicate butterflies as big as her palm. She resisted the temptation and scrambled on, yelling at Alfie and Mia to wait for her by the waterfall – the family's source of fresh water on the island.

'Hurry up, slowcoach.' Mia danced on the spot while Alfie sat on a rock and dipped his feet in the cool water. Their climb was almost over – after another few feet of scrabbling for footholds they'd have reached the top.

'We have to choose the best spot for the lookout.' Now Fleur took the lead.

'With a clear view,' Alfie agreed.

'Just a bit further.' Fleur knew that they had to stop short of the thick jungle where they hardly ever ventured. It covered the misty, mysterious peak of the mountain. 'We wouldn't be able to see anything for branches and creepers if we went as far as the trees.'

So they climbed the slope a little way and chose a ledge of rock at the edge of the jungle – one with a wide, clear view of the sea below. A fresh breeze blew.

'This is it,' Fleur decided. 'We can see for miles.'

'And we won't even need to build a platform,' Alfie decided.

'Oh and look!' Mia pointed out across the bay at a sight they'd been hoping for all day.

Half a dozen dolphins played in the water, riding the rising waves, cresting them before twisting and leaping clear. They were tiny shapes in the distance but unmistakable with their grey, curved backs and pale flanks, their sickle-shaped dorsal fins and strong forked tails.

'Oh, wow!' The sight made Alfie's heartbeat quicken. The dolphins were playing in the waves, rising vertically out of the water then flipping backwards, or riding the swell on their bellies like surfers poised and waiting for that moment when the wave broke and sped them forward in a burst of white spray. Then one dolphin reappeared to clear the water in an acrobatic arc before plunging down out of sight again. Others followed – a pair of them in unison, twisting in the air and disappearing, then up again for pure joy.

Fleur raised both arms and waved. 'I bet they can see us, even from that far away,' she said with a laugh. 'I expect they're wondering what we're up to.'

'We'll tell them later,' Alfie said with a grin.

A puzzled Mia stared at her older brother and sister. She spread her palms upwards. 'Uh, remember – dolphins can't talk!' They might click their throats and whistle through their blowholes in what sounded like excited chatter, but they couldn't say real words.

Alfie winked at Fleur then grinned at Mia. 'What makes you say that?'

''Cos they can't.' Everyone knew it. Yes, dolphins were mega-clever and friendly and sometimes they even saved people's lives. But no way could they actually speak.

Alfie cocked his head to one side and grinned at her from under the brim of his hat. 'I betcha two cockatoo feathers they can!'

'Can't!' she insisted.

'Can,' he teased as Fleur turned to the job in hand and dragged the two of them off to gather wood that they could use to build a lookout fire.

*

An hour later, Fleur, Alfie and Mia had collected every scrap of wood they could find from the slope leading up to the jungle. They had a small pile of broken branches and a tangle of withered grass and creepers that they could use as kindling when they were ready to start the fire.

'It's not enough,' Alfie said with a frown. 'We need more.'

'Let's fetch some from the jungle.' Mia wasn't scared of going in there – to her it was another adventure.

Fleur wasn't sure. 'It's really dark in there,' she warned. 'You can't see where you're going. You could easily trip and hurt yourself.'

'Plus – spiders live there,' Alfie said with a shudder. 'Big, hairy ones – maybe poisonous.'

'Scorpions,' Fleur added. 'Rats and toads and snakes.'

'But we'd find loads of logs and things for the fire.'

Mia refused to be put off.

Alfie decided she was right – they had to try. He glanced at Fleur. 'Maybe just on the edge? We wouldn't have to go in very far.'

'I'm the only one who's been in there, remember? It's really dark and creepy. You can hear things moving but you can't see them.'

'Scaredy-cats.' Mia marched on up the slope – a small figure in a turquoise T-shirt, garlanded with seashell necklaces. She reached the edge of the jungle.

'Come on – we can't let her go in there by herself,' Alfie decided. He scrambled after her and overtook her, aware that Fleur followed more slowly. The sun was on his back but the way ahead was thick with shadows. Wind rustled the leaves of overhanging trees and there were other sounds too – of branches creaking and lianas swaying, and perhaps of creatures moving stealthily through thick undergrowth. He felt goose bumps on his bare arms and the hairs on the back of his neck stood on end.

'Now do you believe me?' Fleur said as she joined Alfie and Mia, who hovered on the edge of the jungle.

'You can't even see the ground in front of you. You have to balance on those big tree roots on the surface and feel your way along.'

Slowly their eyes got used to the shadows. They made out the thick tree trunks rising high overhead, their branches intertwined to make a dark canopy with tiny glimmers of sunlight shining through. Creepers as thick as their arms looped down from the branches and gnarled roots splayed out in all directions. Every nook and cranny could give a home to a skink, a possum or worse. Every branch was a perfect perch for flying foxes to hang from.

'I'm still not scared,' Mia declared. Seeing a fallen branch, she began to edge forward.

Fleur clenched her fists and gritted her teeth. 'Wait. I'll help you,' she muttered.

Now it was Alfie's turn to hang back. He didn't mind about bats – he was used to them from the first night they'd spent in George's cave. He didn't care about skinks or other small reptiles like geckos and lizards – actually he quite liked the fact that they looked like mini-dinosaurs. What stopped him from following the girls was a strong sense that there was something else here in the jungle – a silent presence watching their every move.

'Yuck!' Mia gave a cry as her foot slipped from the root she was balancing on. It squelched into a wet, foul-smelling swamp that oozed around her ankle and refused to let her go.

'Don't move.' Fleur crouched down to pull Mia's foot free. There was a sucking sound and Mia gave a sigh of relief.

Eyes were watching them – Alfie felt sure of it. He looked up into the high branches for tree kangaroos – reddish-brown animals with long thick tails that helped them balance. They weren't real kangaroos but everyone called them that. No – there was nothing staring back at him. Perhaps closer to the ground – there might be a wild boar in here. Alfie had seen them on other islands they'd visited before the shipwreck – boars loved to forage on the dark forest floor. But they made loud snorts and grunts as they blundered through the undergrowth and whatever was watching him, Mia and Fleur made no noise.

'Help us with this, Alfie.' Fleur tugged at the broken branch Mia had spotted. One end was wedged under a large stone.

So reluctantly he made his way further into the shadows and helped to pull the branch free. The movement disturbed a big, black rat that shot out from behind the stone and scuttled along the root where they all balanced.

Fleur jumped with fright then quickly regained control. 'OK, Alfie – you take that end. I'll carry the other. Mia, you make sure you don't slip.'

Slowly they headed out of the shadows into the light. They were almost there when Alfie felt something sharp hit him on the shoulder. It made him wince and he looked up quickly.

'Hey!' The same thing had happened to Mia. 'Who did that?'

It felt like a small stone, thrown from a great height. One, two, three, four in quick succession. *Ouch! Ouch! Ouch!*

Fleur, Mia and Alfie let the branch drop to the ground and covered their heads with their arms. They were being pelted with hard brown nuts from one of the trees and whatever was throwing them had a good aim.

'Hey, stop that!' Mia cried as she crouched low.

There was a chattering noise and lots of movement in the branches above their heads. Then three brown shapes swung down through the creepers to take a closer look at the intruders. Their eyes were large and dark in their grey faces and tufts of reddish brown hair sprouted from their foreheads.

'Bad monkeys!' Mia yelled when she saw who had been throwing nuts at them.

Fleur stood up and laughed out loud in relief. Only monkeys – thank heavens for that.

Soon the first three culprits were joined by almost a dozen more – macaques of all sizes, young and old. They surrounded their visitors, running nimbly along roots and swinging from low creepers, squeaking and chattering at them to shoo them back into the daylight.

'It's OK, they won't hurt us,' Fleur reassured Mia and Alfie. They were so cute and amazing to watch – better than any acrobat you saw on TV.

'They already did.' Alfie rubbed his shoulder where the first nut had hit. There were monkeys everywhere you looked, mothers running down tree trunks with young ones clinging to their backs, adult males leaping from root to root, keeping up their wild squealing and chattering.

'OK, let's leave the branch where it is,' Fleur decided. 'We can come back for it later when the monkeys have gone.'

Yay!' Mia cried. There were real live monkeys here on Dolphin Island to make up for her toy one that had sunk with *Merlin*. 'Bags I tell Mum and Dad. Last one down to the beach is a dummy!'

Chapter Three

In the glow of the setting sun later that day, Alfie swam with Pearl. She ploughed through the water towards him, head tilted back and showing him her pearly pink underside, clicking out a greeting especially for him.

'Finally!' he cried, spreading his arms wide and laughing as she suddenly dipped out of sight. He felt the water swirl beneath him and waited for her to pop up again to say hello. But no – Pearl was playing the game of blowing bubble rings from under the surface, waiting for him to dive down and join her. He kicked his legs and thrust his body deep underwater, keeping his eyes wide open to see the bubbles rise.

Up above water, Fleur and Mia played with Jazz and Stormy. The dolphins swam side by side with just enough space between them for one of the girls to take hold of their flippers.

'Me first!' Mia whooped with delight as she held on and the dolphins propelled her forward through the waves.

'Hang on tight,' Fleur called after her.

Mia got a mouthful of salty water. She felt Stormy and Jazz slow down then turn. Back they sped towards Fleur, as fast as before. At the end of the ride they broke apart with a side roll and a flip of their mighty tails.

'Now me.' Fleur stroked Jazz's head as he swam back, then she kissed the top of Stormy's head. 'Ready,' she said as she grabbed their fins and looked straight ahead.

Whoosh! The pair accelerated fast, setting up a bow-wave that thrust Fleur's head back with the force of the water. Unlike Mia, she kept her eyes and mouth tight shut. Out to sea they swam swiftly then slowed and turned. Back again at full speed, giving Fleur the ride of her life.

'That was fun,' Mia called out to Alfie who was now sitting astride Pearl's back to hitch a lift back to shore.

The sun had almost disappeared behind the horizon

and before long the three dolphins were saying their goodbyes. They gathered in the shallow waves, each giving their special whistle. Pearl's was a quick succession of bird-like chirps, while Stormy gave a single shrill call and Jazz gave his signature high-low, high-low farewell. Mia, Fleur and Alfie hugged them then watched them set off on an evening fishing expedition, clapping their jaws together as they went.

'Who says they can't talk?' Alfie gave Mia a mischievous grin. There weren't enough words to describe how much he'd enjoyed teaming up with Pearl – he just loved every second.

The swim had washed away the day's worries. Mia, Alfie and Fleur had returned from the jungle covered in bruises from the nuts the monkeys had thrown at them and described what had happened to their mum and dad.

'We always knew it could be dangerous in there,' James had said from his 'hospital' hammock.

'The trouble is – we don't know what might be living in the jungle besides monkeys,' Katie had agreed.

The warning had struck a deep chord in Alfie's lively

imagination but he'd kept quiet while Fleur had insisted that the macaques were sweet and funny and Mia had declared that she wanted one as a pet.

'No more pets,' James had ordered. 'One gecko mouth to feed is quite enough.'

For the rest of the day they'd collected driftwood that was small enough to carry on their shoulders up to the new lookout at the top of the cliff. By the end of a tiring afternoon this had amounted to a big pile of dry kindling. A plan was then made to return to camp and spend some quiet time making shell necklaces before a final swim in the sea.

'We'll light the new fire in the daylight tomorrow,' Katie had decided. 'Climbing up and down the cliff is tricky in the dark.'

Lastly they'd enjoyed a swim with the dolphins, which had rounded off their day and brought Alfie out of his shell.

'Feeling better now?' Fleur asked as they meandered up the beach towards camp.

The seawater felt prickly as it dried quickly on his skin. The sand still felt warm underfoot. 'Yeah, cool,' he replied.

'You were quiet earlier.'

He tutted and glanced at Mia who was whooping and performing cartwheels on the sand. 'That makes up for someone else I know.' He didn't tell Fleur the truth about how afraid he'd been in the jungle or about the thoughts that kept buzzing around inside his head. Or how he couldn't help remembering the telescope that Granddad Tony had in a spare bedroom through which Alfie could gaze at the stars, the science books on his bedroom shelf and his favourite computer games – things from home that constantly tugged at his heart.

So he stayed quiet and thoughtful, lagging behind Fleur, lost in his memories and fears.

*

'Day 9!' Mia marked the calendar stick with a piece of charcoal.

'Uh-huh-huh,' Fleur groaned. 'Too early. Go back to sleep.'

Ignoring her, Mia left the shelter to find Alfie already up and tending the fire. 'What are we going to do today?' she asked him.

'Light the lookout fire,' he reminded her. 'Then one of us will have to stay up there and keep watch.'

'Me first!' Mia took a gulp of water straight from Alfie's plastic bottle then hopped on to the nearby raft – a cane platform tied to four large white containers that raised it thirty centimetres off the ground and acted as flotation aids when they took it out to sea. Mia started to bounce up and down.

'Watch out – that's not a bouncy castle. It'll break if you're not careful,' Alfie warned.

Too late – there was the sound of bamboo canes splitting. 'Oops!'

Alfie tutted but said nothing. Instead he made a mental note – *put mending the raft on the list of jobs to do today.*

Undeterred, Mia jumped down then went exploring in the bushes behind the shelter. She came back with dry leaves tangled in her hair and holding up a new feather.

'Wow – let's see!' Fleur had decided to come out and see what damage Mia had done to the raft.

Mia showed her a long, curved feather of iridescent

blue. It was an exciting new item to add to her collection.

'Bird of paradise.' Straight away Fleur recognized what Mia had found. The male of the species was her favourite bird – a strutting show-off who fanned out his shiny tail feathers to attract a mate. He had a funny tuft on his head and a red wattle hanging from his beak that wobbled when he stretched his neck then dipped his beak. 'Mia, that's amazing.'

Proudly Mia disappeared into the tent to fix her latest find into her hat band.

'How did you sleep?' Fleur asked Alfie.

He blew out through his lips – a sound that meant *Don't ask*.

'Any dolphins this morning?'

'Nope.'

Fleur scanned the sea then switched her attention to the headlands to either side of their bay. 'Guess what?' she said. 'We've got other visitors.'

Alfie looked up from his fire duties to see a band of monkeys scampering over the rocks to the west. There were about twelve of them foraging in rock pools, scooping up small fish and crabs.

'I'm going to take a closer look.' Fleur set off at a jog across the beach, hoping that the monkeys would be too busy to notice her. She got close enough to see them picking up sharp stones and using them to crack open the shells of the crabs they'd caught. 'Amazing,' she said again, slowing down and approaching more cautiously. She watched a female open up a crab and prise out the meat to give to her youngster who gobbled it down greedily.

It was only when Mia cantered along the beach to join her that the monkeys realized anyone was there.

'Yee-hah!' Mia slapped her thigh as if she was urging a pony into a gallop.

The monkeys looked up in alarm. In a split second they jumped down the far side of the headland and disappeared.

'Aaagh!' Fleur put her hands to her head. 'Mia, I was watching the monkeys!'

'Oops!' Mia said again.

*

After breakfast, the Fisher children set about the task

of collecting coconuts and scooping fish out of the shallow water with their canvas 'net'. The dolphins had first shown them how to do this by corralling a silvery shoal in a rocky inlet. Seizing their chance, Fleur, Alfie and Mia had used a piece of canvas to form a barrier that prevented the fish from swimming back out to sea. With care and patience, they might catch up to a dozen – enough for lunch and dinner. After a successful expedition, Katie said they could at last think about lighting the new lookout fire.

'What's to think about?' an impatient Fleur asked. 'Don't we just go up there and do it?'

'I've got a better idea.' As usual, Alfie had planned ahead. 'It takes ages to rub sticks together to make a spark. So why don't we take fire from here up the cliff with us instead?'

Fleur didn't see how it would work. 'Wouldn't the wind blow the flames out on the way up?'

'Not if we make a proper torch,' Alfie said. He walked a little way down the beach and brought back a coconut cup that he'd stored safely behind a rock. 'Out of this,' he explained.

'Yuck!' Mia took a quick sniff at some gooey black stuff inside the cup then backed away. 'What is it?'

'It's oil that got spilled from a tanker,' Alfie told them. 'I know – it's horrible when it gets washed ashore. You have to be careful not to stand in it 'cos you can never get it off the soles of your feet.'

'But tar burns easily.' Fleur saw what he was getting at.

He nodded. 'What we do is cover some dry brushwood with this, tie it to a pole to make a sort of broom then set light to it from our fire down here. Ta-dah, a proper torch!'

'Clever!' James's voice encouraged them. He sounded weak and tired, but determined to give his opinion.

'It's worth a try,' Katie agreed.

So they followed Alfie's idea, taking care not to dirty their hands and to make sure that the brushwood was heavily coated with the gloopy black tar before they thrust it into the flames. The brushwood flared into life, giving off a thick, evil-smelling smoke.

'OK, let's go.' Immediately Alfie set off with Fleur

following, leaving Mia behind for safety.

'It's not fair. Why can't I go?' she pestered, looking longingly at the blazing torch that Alfie carried.

'Because,' Katie told her firmly.

It felt exciting to be carrying fire. Alfie was pleased with how well his idea had worked. He held the flaming torch aloft, hearing it spit and crackle as he climbed the steep cliff with ease.

'Not far now,' Fleur promised. 'Honestly, Alfie – you're amazing.'

'Everything is "amazing" with you today,' he laughed as he climbed.

Five minutes later they reached their lookout platform. The pyramid of driftwood was still there and Alfie didn't waste time. Making sure that the wind would blow the flames away from him and Fleur, he pushed the torch into the centre. Within seconds the fire was alight and smoke rose high in the sky.

Alfie and Fleur grinned at each other. Their mission was accomplished.

But they needed more wood, so Fleur left Alfie to tend the fire and scrambled up the slope to fetch the branch they'd left behind on the day before. This time she didn't stop to think about the dark jungle interior and what might be lurking. Her job was to fetch the branch and keep the fire going. Balancing like a tightrope walker along the gnarled roots, she brushed aside cobwebs and low-hanging creepers and forged ahead.

Was this the right place? she wondered. All the trees looked alike and it was hard to see more than a few steps ahead. But then she spotted the abandoned branch and a second one just a few metres away. At this rate, they would have enough firewood to last at least the rest of the day. Already panting from the effort of climbing, her face started to run with sweat as she seized the first branch and began to drag it clear of the forest.

She emerged blinking into the daylight to see Alfie still crouched by the fire, fanning the flames with his hat.

'It nearly went out,' he explained as she lugged the branch down the slope. 'It's OK now though.'

'More than OK,' she agreed. Orange flames licked

hungrily at the pyramid, making the wood resin bubble and spit. Alfie's tar torch had done its job well.

'I've spotted another branch. Why don't you try breaking this one into smaller pieces while I go back for it?'

They worked like this through the rest of the morning so that by midday there was a good supply of firewood. By now the sun scorched their backs and it was too hot to carry on.

'We need a drink,' Alfie decided, accidentally smudging his face with charcoal dust that made him look like a miner emerging from a coal mine. The whites of his eyes stood out against his blackened cheeks.

So they went to the waterfall together to drink and dip their feet in the tumbling stream.

'Let me stay and watch the fire – you go down and have a rest,' Alfie suggested.

Fleur was too tired to argue. 'I'll come back and take over when the sun is halfway down in the west,' she decided. Without watches or phones, the progress of the sun in the sky was the only way to keep track of the time. 'Are you sure you'll be OK?'

'Go,' he insisted. The job of keeping the fire going suited him – it gave him a chance to daydream without any interruptions from Mia.

'Keep a good lookout for ships.' Fleur started to pick her way down the cliff. A clear turquoise sea spread at her feet, with patches of darker blue showing where the coral reefs were. The waves broke gently on to a white beach. When she glanced back, she saw that Alfie was already back on the rocky ledge next to their new fire, squatting down on his haunches, his hat low over his face. He looked lonely and small perched up there on his own. She waved up at him and he waved back.

Stay safe, Alfie, she thought as she carried on picking her way down the cliff.

Chapter Four

'I wonder what else we'll find to eat on Dolphin Island.' Fleur lay inside the shelter on her palm leaf matting, daydreaming about food.

'Yeah – besides yucky fish and coconuts.' Forced to take a siesta, Mia was threading more shells on to a piece of fishing line rescued from the rubbish that got washed up on to the beach. This time it was for a bracelet for her mum.

'We have yummy jackfruit,' James reminded them from his hammock.

'What about bananas?' Fleur wondered. 'Now that we know there are monkeys here, that means we might find bananas in the jungle.'

'Maybe.' Katie sounded thoughtful. She knew a lot about how things grew in the tropics from a college course she taught on global warming. 'You know we're hundreds of miles from civilization and no one has ever lived here or planted food crops, but seeds do arrive on these islands in many different ways. They're carried in the air or in birds' stomachs, or sometimes they're simply washed up from passing boats.'

'That means there could be other stuff like sugarcane, berries, yams, breadfruit ...' Fleur, who liked to look on the bright side, made a grocery list of what they might find.

'Sugar – yummy!' Mia said with a sigh.

'We definitely know there are nuts,' Fleur pointed out. 'That's what the monkeys threw at us yesterday.'

'It's worth checking out later today,' Katie agreed.

The conversation wandered from nuts to crabs and seaweed. Katie said there were certain types of seaweed that were good to eat, but it was hard to know which ones.

'Seaweed – yuck,' Mia said with a yawn.

Fleur looked up and spotted George clinging to the ceiling, his stick-like legs crooked, his long toes spread wide. 'Hey,' she murmured.

George flicked out his tongue and caught a tasty insect.

'Thanks – that's one less bug for us to be bitten by,' Fleur commented. 'I wonder how Alfie's getting on. Maybe I should go and find out?'

*

I wish, *I wish I could forget about being shipwrecked!*

Up on the ledge, in the full heat and glare of the sun, Alfie clenched his fists. The sea below was calm and blue, yet all he could think of was giant, rolling waves tossing him up and down, up and down – and black clouds and cold mist, winds tearing at *Merlin*'s sails. He heard again the water slapping and thudding against the boat's hull and felt himself being tossed overboard like a rag doll. Pitched over the guardrail by a violent lurch of the boat to starboard, trying to cling on, failing and falling – down, down into the sea.

Don't think about it! he told himself. *Look out for dolphins, concentrate on nice things.*

He put wood on the fire then searched the bay. A few white clouds gathered over a distant headland – a sign that rain might be on its way. But Pearl and the others were nowhere to be seen.

Feed the fire, keep a lookout. Don't think about the downward plunge into murky water with your lungs almost bursting, the pull of the current dragging you down.

'Hey,' Fleur greeted him as if out of nowhere.

Alfie hadn't noticed her climb the cliff or cross the slope. 'You made me jump,' he complained. 'How was your siesta?'

'Cool. I dreamed about bananas.' She gave him one of her wide smiles and tucked stray strands of hair under her hat. 'How is it up here?'

'Windy,' he admitted. 'And I think it's going to rain.'

They looked, and sure enough, over on the distant headland, the clouds were thickening and turning from white to grey. Meanwhile, in the middle of the bay, their dolphins appeared. It was the whole pod – Stormy, Pearl and Jazz, together with three other young calves and their mothers who watched the young ones play in the rising swell of waves.

'They're a long way out,' Fleur remarked. 'That's what they do when a storm is due – they stay clear of the rocks.'

She and Alfie watched a while, cheered up as usual by the sight of the youngsters lob-tailing and twisting, leaping and flipping seaweed into the air from their snouts and tails. Then, all too soon, their mothers swam in to halt their play. The adults paired up with their calves and led them further out to sea until the pod dwindled to grey specks bobbing up and down in the waves.

Quickly the clouds drew in. The wind grew stronger, bringing with it cold splashes of rain that hissed as they fell into the fire.

'Why didn't we think of this?' Alfie was angry with himself. He should've worked out what to do up here when it rained – maybe made some sort of shelter out of palm leaves to protect both themselves and the fire.

'Come on – let's build it up as much as we can.' Fleur set to work. With luck the rain would blow over quickly, like a lot of tropical storms.

Alfie helped her to pile wood on to the fire, but he did it half-heartedly. He'd worked out that ships would do what the dolphins had just done – that is, they would change course to stay well away from land and dangerous rocks until the storm was over. Anyway, a thick mist was descending – so what good was a smoke signal when no one could see more than a few metres ahead of them?

'Come on, Alfie – we can do this,' Fleur urged. The rain came down hard now, dousing the flames. It had soaked through their T-shirts and their hair was dripping wet.

They went on feeding the fire but the flames grew weaker and the embers beneath the fresh logs turned slowly from red to grey. The wind tore at their hats and lashed their faces, arms and legs.

'It's no good – we can't keep it alight.' Alfie flung aside a piece of wood in disgust.

The heavy rain built to a downpour. The fire hissed and died.

Fleur gave in and sat down heavily, letting her legs dangle over the edge of the ledge. She bowed her head and felt the rain prick the skin on her neck and shoulders.

'It's useless.' Alfie stood a little way off, lost in the

mist. 'I'm useless. This was a terrible idea.'

'No, don't say that. We can build another fire,' Fleur argued. Right now, though, she felt exhausted.

'It's not worth it.' As he shook his head, rain streamed down his face and mingled with the tears that he couldn't hold back. Nothing worked. The Fishers were doomed to stay on Dolphin Island for ever.

*

'We're a team – we never give up,' James told Alfie and Fleur after they'd got back to camp, appearing like two drowned rats out of the grey mist.

The rain eased and the sky brightened. Within half an hour the sky would be blue again. Hearing their voices, James had struggled out of his hammock and come to sit with them as Katie and Mia fought to keep the main fire burning.

'Look how well we've done so far,' James reminded them as he studied Alfie's smudged, unhappy face. 'We haven't starved and we haven't died of thirst. Every day we find something that makes our lives better. What day is it today?'

'Day 9,' Mia yelled as she dragged a piece of driftwood close to the fire. 'Check the calendar stick, Dad!'

'Do you hear what I'm saying, Alfie? We keep our chins up whatever happens.'

Alfie nodded but didn't look up to meet his dad's gaze. He didn't know if he really believed him.

'So.' James ignored the pain it cost him to reach out and put his arm around Alfie's shoulder. 'The storm is passing and we'll soon be back to normal. Tomorrow is another day.'

*

Day 10. Alfie looked out of the shelter at their main fire still alight and a beach still pockmarked with yesterday's raindrops. The sky was blue and the sun well up in the sky.

'Hey, lazy-bones.' Fleur was already awake and hanging her T-shirt from a bush to dry.

Mia was practising handstands against the upturned raft that Alfie had mended.

'How did you sleep?' Fleur asked.

'Fine,' he lied as he crawled out of the shelter. He

didn't want to talk so he wandered down to the rocks where a small white object immediately caught his attention. He stooped and picked it up.

It was a pair of sunglasses, still with their lenses in – a bit scratched but not cracked. In fact, he knew who they belonged to – they were Fleur's favourite sporty ones.

How did they get here? Alfie wondered, a sudden flicker of interest pulling him out of his gloomy mood. Fleur hadn't been wearing them when *Merlin* had sunk and she hadn't rescued them when they'd rowed out there on the raft. So they must have been washed up from under the sea during yesterday's storm.

And wait – what was that, tangled up in slimy brown seaweed? Alfie bent down again and picked up a yellow tube of sunscreen – the kind they'd kept on board. It would definitely be useful, he decided as he shoved it into his pocket. He was about to set off back for camp with his finds when he stooped again to dislodge a larger object from a crevice in the rocks. This time it was a dark blue backpack, dripping wet but still intact. Jumping down from the rocks with his heart beating fast, he set the bag on the sand and unzipped it.

It was full of clothes that his mum must have set aside for washing. There were sodden T-shirts and shorts, skirts, dresses, knickers and underpants, plus Alfie's own spare swimming shorts and the girls' swimsuits. *Wow!* He jumped up and yelled at Fleur and Mia to come quick.

'What's he found?' Mia didn't wait for Fleur to answer. Off she shot across the beach.

Whatever it was, Alfie sounded excited so Fleur took off after Mia. They arrived at the same time to find him surrounded by … laundry!

'Oh my gosh, clothes – *real* clothes!' Fleur gasped with delight.

'Here's my Cinderella swimmie!' Mia seized her much loved Disney swimsuit and swung it in the air. She did a victory dance on the sand.

Alfie handed Fleur her sunglasses and grinned when she put them on.

'Now I'm a tourist again!' she giggled. 'Well done, Alfie. Mum and Dad will be really pleased. Thank you, thank you. There's lots of mega cool stuff here.'

'Don't thank me – thank yesterday's storm. It must have churned stuff up below the surface and then the currents dumped this lot on the rocks.'

'That means there might be more things if we carry on looking.' Beside herself with excitement, Fleur hightailed it back to the shelter to pass on the good news while Mia changed into a damp Minnie Mouse T-shirt and a frilly white skirt.

'What else is in here?' she demanded, delving into the backpack and producing her dad's blue-striped shirt. Beneath that, at the bottom of the bag, her fingers made contact with something soggy and soft. Gingerly she drew it out and turned it over in her hands.

It was a small, squidgy brown thing that at first she didn't recognize. It definitely wasn't more clothes, that was for sure.

'What did you find?' Alfie peered over her shoulder.

The thing had a head and a body and a long tail. It had small round ears and a smiley face.

'Monkey!' Mia recognized the sodden soft toy. He was her favourite and she remembered how she'd spilled baked beans on him and he'd been put in with the laundry. But then *Merlin* had sunk and she'd thought she'd lost him for ever. Now she squeezed him and hugged him and swore she would never let him go. 'Monkey!' she yelled as she ran up the beach as fast as her legs would carry her. 'Alfie found Monkey – look, everyone. Look!'

Chapter Five

The first thing that Alfie did after he carried the bag of clothes back to the shelter was to climb the cliff and start work on rebuilding the lookout fire.

'That's the spirit,' his dad told him as he watched him set off. He was relieved to see that Alfie had got over the disappointment of yesterday and was willing to try again. 'I only wish I could come with you.'

In truth, though James didn't admit it to anyone, he had a splitting headache and when he tried to sit up he felt as weak as a kitten.

'Don't even think about it, Dad.' Fleur jumped up to follow Alfie. 'I'll go.'

She easily caught up with him and they talked about how they would go back into the jungle for more wood and this time they would also work out how to build a canopy to shield the fire from the rain.

'Wouldn't a canopy catch fire though?' Fleur pictured red sparks shooting upwards and setting light to anything made from branches and woven palm leaves.

'But we can't just let the lookout fire go out every time it rains,' Alfie insisted as they rested by the waterfall. 'It's too much trouble to rebuild it afterwards.'

Standing with hands on hips, scanning the slope ahead, Fleur picked out a better place fifty metres to the left of where they'd built the fire the first time – a ledge with an overhang that formed a shallow cave in the rock face. 'How about there?' she asked.

Alfie nodded eagerly. 'It's further from camp, but if we build it there, the rock will make a roof so we won't need to build one ourselves. And rock doesn't catch fire.'

They agreed on the new spot and began the slow task of collecting more firewood, working hard until the heat of the sun slowed them down and forced them to take a rest under the trees at the edge of the jungle.

'Phew!' Fleur took off her hat and fanned her face.

Slowly she grew aware that they weren't the only ones to seek the shade. 'Look!' she hissed, pointing five metres up into the branches at three curious monkeys who sat and stared down at them.

'And over there.' Alfie saw two more monkeys scamper across the bare slope below. They ran on all fours, bounding over boulders, the sun shining fiercely on their heads and backs. When they reached the jungle, they stopped short, stood upright, bared their teeth and glared at the uninvited human visitors.

'Yes, it's us – we're back,' Fleur said with a smile.

Overhead, the three monkeys chattered excitedly.

'We won't hurt you,' she promised.

'They don't know that though.' Alfie spoke warily. He didn't fancy being bitten by an angry monkey.

Luckily, the two on the ground decided to skirt around the side of Alfie and Fleur before disappearing into the thick undergrowth. After some loud rustling, they reappeared beside the three on the branch and all five stared down.

'What now?' Alfie was afraid they were about to be pelted with nuts again.

'Aw, look – they're grooming.' Fleur watched the monkeys lose interest in her and Alfie and start to pick at each other's fur with nimble fingers and fixed concentration. 'So cute!' she breathed.

But the macaques were not so cute when, half an hour later, Fleur had dragged a branch down the slope then gone to the stream for a drink. She took off her newly rescued sunglasses, put them on a rock and bent over the water with cupped hands. 'Hey!' she shouted as, in the blink of an eye, a monkey darted out from behind a rock and pinched the glasses.

He picked them up and ran with them to a safe distance. Then he sat and examined the shiny white and black object.

Fleur followed cautiously. 'They're mine. Alfie only just found them for me.'

The monkey turned the glasses over. He sniffed them then tapped the lenses against the rock.

Fleur cringed. 'Please don't break them.'

They didn't smell good, the monkey thought, and they made a strange rattling sound. He tilted his head to one side and looked quizzically at Fleur.

What use are these?

'Don't!' she begged as, with a toothy grin, he raised the glasses above his head and tossed them wildly in the air.

Fleur ran without a hope of being able to catch them. She saw where the sunglasses landed. With a sinking feeling she bent to pick them up.

The lenses were cracked, the hinges broken. 'Oh,' she groaned, shaking her fist at the monkey thief as he scuttled away. 'And I thought you were my friend.'

*

By the end of the day the hard work was done. There was a new lookout fire on the mountain and fresh fish for supper followed by mouthwatering jackfruit collected from the edge of the jungle.

'It's my turn to keep a lookout,' Katie decided as she, Alfie, Mia and James sat around the campfire licking their fingers. 'I'll do the overnight shift. Mia – hands off that fruit – we've saved it for Fleur.'

'G'night, Mum!'

'Goodnight. Sleep well.'

Feeling lazy, Alfie and Mia lounged at the entrance

to the shelter in the gathering dusk, waiting for Fleur to arrive.

'Here I am,' she declared as she emerged from the bushes. A cane toad hopped clumsily out of her way. 'What's for supper?'

'Jelly and ice cream,' Mia said with a giggle. Then she challenged Alfie to a race to the shore. 'First one to see dolphins …!'

'That girl never sits still.' James rose stiffly to his feet. He swayed and almost fell.

'Dad, are you all right?' Alarmed, Fleur ran to support him. Sweat ran down his pale face. 'You look awful.'

'I'm fine,' he insisted, clutching his ribs as he went inside and eased himself on to his hammock. 'Why don't you save your supper for later and join the others?'

So Fleur walked slowly down the beach, her light brown eyes clouded with worry. She tried not to think about what would happen if their dad didn't start to get better soon – on Dolphin Island there were certainly no doctors to call on and no medicine to take.

Pretty soon Jazz came and helped put her fears to one side. He appeared in the silvery waves with Stormy and Pearl as the sun went down. All three were ready to play.

'This is my best time of day,' Mia said with a happy sigh. She swam up to meet Stormy and stroked his white belly.

He clacked his teeth together. *Do that again!*

She laughed and stroked him, then they rolled together in the white surf until Stormy broke free and whistled at her. Mia clapped her hands with delight.

Fleur meanwhile had thrown her arms around Jazz for his favourite cuddle then sat astride his back. He set off across the bay, riding the waves and giving her a rollercoaster ride until they reached the rocks where *Merlin* had sunk. He circled them slowly.

'I know,' she sighed, leaning forward to give him another hug. 'The boat's gone. It's sad, isn't it?'

Jazz clicked a reply then returned her slowly to shore where Alfie sat in the shallows with Pearl.

'Aren't you coming in for a swim?' Fleur asked.

'Not today.' Alfie didn't feel like going out of his depth.

Pearl seemed to understand this and swam in slow circles, playfully splashing water at him with her tail flukes until her mother, Marina, showed up and gave the calves the signal that it was time for them to leave.

'It'll soon be dark,' Fleur realized as they stood ankle-deep in the water and waved goodbye. Up on the cliff, the lookout fire flared brightly in the shadows, while here on the beach, pelicans landed on the rocks and storm petrels swooped and fluttered over rock

pools. All was calm in the grey dusk light.

Mia yawned and came to stand beside Fleur. For once she didn't want to race so instead they wandered hand in hand towards camp.

Alfie stayed to watch the dolphins depart. He knew he shouldn't have been afraid to go deeper in the water with Pearl – she always looked after him and would never lead him into danger. So what was wrong with him? Why hadn't he wanted to swim with their dolphin friends like gentle, nature-loving Fleur and madcap Mia?

Maybe he was tired. Yes – that was it. Nightmares had kept him awake last night and he'd had a tough day rebuilding the lookout fire. He needed to sleep.

His feet dragged as he set off up the beach, picking his way through mounds of pink, yellow and brown seaweed thrown up by the storm. He trod on the spikes of a hidden conch shell and stopped to examine his sore foot, putting it down gingerly and limping on until he trod on something else that was solid beneath the tangle of salt-smelling weed. This time it wasn't curved and spiky – it was flat and smooth. He stooped to part the seaweed then picked up a square black object, recognizing it straight away as the router for their broadband equipment on *Merlin*. It was part of a sophisticated network system that had helped them navigate and log their speed and wind direction, plus the precise depth of the waters they were sailing through. Now it was waterlogged and useless – another unhappy reminder of the disaster that had befallen them.

Alfie frowned and put the router back down. He shook his head, sighed and was about to trudge on when he made out a second box poking out from the messy pile of debris. He almost left it where it was until he realized that it was red and shiny, which meant that it hadn't been in the sea long enough for it to get faded and bashed about. Perhaps it would be useful after all.

He pushed the weed aside with his foot. The watertight red container was made of plastic and marked with a big white cross. *Merlin*'s first-aid box – that's what this was! It was where they'd kept bandages and sticking plaster, antiseptic cream, anti-malaria tablets, aspirins and a dozen other medicines he didn't know the names of.

Alfie fell to his knees and grabbed it, shaking it to make sure no water had got inside. Just wait until he told the others! Up he sprang, tucked the box under his arm and began to run.

Chapter Six

Alfie, Mia and Fleur squatted close to the fire so that they could examine the contents of the red box in the flickering light cast by the flames. There was a smell of wood smoke in the air and the ever present sound of the waves.

'What are you lot whispering about out there?' their dad asked from inside the shelter. All day he'd lain in his hammock, too weak to move.

'Nothing!' they chorused.

Keeping quiet meant that Alfie could make certain that the medicines inside the box hadn't been ruined by salt water before they told their dad about them. He took out rolls of bandage and placed them on a flat rock, then some spray cans and tubes of antiseptic. So far everything seemed to be in good condition.

From the bottom of the box, next to a pair of small scissors and some tweezers, Fleur picked out three blister packs of pills. She squinted to read the labels. Anti-diarrhoea tablets, paracetamol, amoxicillin …

'What are these?' she wondered out loud.

Mia grabbed the pack and ran inside. 'Dad, what's "a mox …", "a moxo killin"?'

'"Amoxicillin"!' Feebly he reached out his hand and took them from her. 'These are antibiotics. Where on earth did you find them?'

'Alfie found them with a lot of other stuff. They were in a box under some seaweed.' From the choking, gasping sounds her dad made, Mia could tell that he must be crying but she didn't understand why. Not knowing what to say, she picked Monkey up from her bed mat and tucked him into the crook of her elbow.

Fleur and Alfie followed Mia into the shelter. It was dark inside so they could just make out that their dad, with tears trickling down his cheeks, was trying to sit up and swing his legs over the side of his hammock.

He had to stop. His ribs were too painful and his forehead ran with sweat.

'Stay there, don't move,' Fleur begged.

Slowly he eased himself back into the hammock. 'These antibiotics could be a life-saver,' he groaned. 'Fleury, fetch me a drink of water – there's a good girl.'

She ran outside and splooshed water into a coconut shell cup ready to take it back inside.

Mia crept out after her. 'Why is Dad crying?' she whispered.

'Because he's happy,' Fleur explained. 'Sometimes grown-ups do that.'

Mia went back into the shelter and watched her dad carefully. 'How will the medicine make you better?' she asked.

'I've got an infection, Mi-mi – that's what's making me so poorly. Like you when you get a case of glue ear, only mine is worse than that,' James explained. 'Hopefully these tablets will sort it out.'

'Cool.' Listening to the conversation, Alfie felt a burst of pride that he'd been the one to find them.

'Here's your water,' Fleur said, coming back in. She kept her hand on the cup to steady it as their dad broke one of the tablets out of its pack then swallowed it down.

He nodded then laid his head back. 'Thank you, son – these are a real life-saver,' he said with a sigh.

Fleur smiled at her brother and Mia threw her arms around his waist and hugged him. 'Alfie, you're amazing,' they said.

*

That night the relief of knowing that their dad was going to get better surrounded Alfie like a warm blanket. For once he slept well and woke long after Mia and Fleur had got up and left the shelter.

'How are you feeling?' he asked his dad.

'My ribs are still sore, but my poor head doesn't ache so much.' Fleur had already been in with water for his second pill and now she and Mia had scaled the cliff to take over lookout duty from Katie. 'Your mum will be over the moon when she hears what's happened.'

'Cool. I'll take the raft and see if I can catch something bigger, further out to sea.'

'OK, but make sure you don't go too far,' his dad insisted. 'The currents can be pretty strong out there, so I need to be able to keep an eye on you.'

'Will do.' In spite of the warning, Alfie didn't see the need to mention his plan of paddling into the next cove. They'd named it Turtle Beach because this was where he and the girls had once seen the waves carry sea turtles on to the sand. Right now the tide was going out so he reckoned there was a better chance of catching bigger crabs in the deeper rock pools on the far side of the headland.

'Good lad. Oh and before you go, could you make sure our store of jackfruit is safe? I heard suspicious noises out there during the night. I think it might have been monkeys.'

Sure enough, when Alfie went outside and checked the canvas cover to their food store, he found it ripped to pieces and bits of fruit rind scattered amongst the bushes. They'd have to be more careful in future – hide the food and pin the canvas down more securely with rocks, he decided. 'You were right,' he called to James. 'The monkeys have nicked the lot.'

We'd better add making a safe place to store food to the usual list of things to do, he thought as he lifted one end of the raft and dragged it down the beach. He was wearing blue shorts from the backpack and a blue and white striped T-shirt, but he had the same handmade hat pulled well down over his face. He'd forgotten to put on sunscreen from the tube that they'd found on the beach so he dropped the raft and hurried back for it.

'That was quick,' James quipped. Already he sounded more like his old self.

'Ha-ha,' Alfie replied. The white cream smelled good and felt cool on his arms and face as he rubbed it in. 'See you later, Dad,' he said as he ran off again.

*

While Alfie fished for crabs, Fleur and Mia kept a lookout from the ledge. They'd passed on to Katie the good news about the antibiotics and she'd hurried back to camp, leaving the girls to collect firewood on the mountain slope.

'This is a brilliant start to the day.' When she arrived at camp Katie's smile lit up her face. She was more relieved than she could say, so she kissed James and sat with him for a while, just holding his hand.

Firewood and fish, eating and sleeping, fending off

monkeys, looking out at the empty ocean and listening to the roar of the waves – everyone settled into the routine on the island they now called home. Thursday was Day 11, Friday Day 12 – carefully marked off by Mia on the calendar stick.

'Much better!' James reported each time Mia, Fleur and Alfie asked how he was. He could sit up more easily and his head didn't swim when he tried to stand. On Friday evening he even sat around the campfire with them while Katie, as usual, took the night shift on the mountain.

Fleur baked crab meat in the embers of the fire – a feast brought back by Alfie from another of his outings on the raft. It was delicious. Then they had roasted coconut with its sweet milk to drink so they went to bed with full stomachs.

'No sign of the dolphins for ages,' Mia sighed. It had been the only downside in her day.

'The weather's calm – that's why. They're probably fishing way out in the ocean.' By now Fleur knew the pod's habits. 'Anyway, they know we can cope without them.'

'But Stormy will come back, won't he?' Mia sounded worried.

In the darkness of the shelter, Alfie listened but said nothing.

'Yes,' Fleur told Mia in a soothing voice. 'He'll be back.'

*

That night Alfie had his worst nightmare ever. It began the same way as usual with mountainous green-black waves breaking over him and crashing down, throwing him on to his stomach. He clutched at the guardrail, missed and was flung to starboard. Another wave smashed on to the boat. White mist blinded him as he slithered over the smooth deck with nothing to hold on to, slipped back a little way as the boat tilted and then again to starboard and over the edge, flipping through the air and hitting the water, vanishing underneath.

Down and down into murky depths, kicking his legs and flailing his arms in a current that dragged him further under. Surrounded by pieces of sinking wreckage – a compass torn from the chart table, plates and cups from the galley, part of a metal chair. In his dark dream, there was no Pearl to rescue him. He sank to the bottom of the sea.

His heart pounding and gasping for air, Alfie jerked awake. He got up from his sleeping mat and stumbled outside. The black sky was sprinkled with a million stars. He, Alfie Fisher, was a tiny speck of dust in a vast universe.

He shivered. Too scared to go back to sleep, he sat by the fire and waited for the dawn.

*

As soon as the sun rose, Alfie left camp. He went down to the sea to look for Pearl.

If only the dolphins would come, he would feel better.

Waves lapped around his ankles as he scanned the far horizon. The water sucked sand from under his feet, making him lose his balance and fall to his knees. He picked himself up and climbed on to the headland. Again he searched for dolphins in vain.

If they wouldn't come, he would wander off by himself, he decided. Rather than go back to camp for breakfast, he would do some beachcombing and hope to pick up more useful objects from the next cove. It was early so the others probably wouldn't even miss him. Anyway, by now he knew his way around.

He faced the wind and scrambled down the rocks on to Turtle Beach. It was a smaller, narrower bay, leading up to a cave hidden by tall grasses and a thicket of bamboo, with the usual curve of rubbish littering the high-tide line. First Alfie picked up driftwood for the fire and began to make a pile, ready to carry back to camp. Then he switched to smaller, man-made stuff – a baked beans can, an old flip-flop, a plastic carrier bag. Most people would hate the litter as an eyesore in what was otherwise Paradise, but Alfie seized on it eagerly, stashing it between two boulders for later. This was the one good thing about the storms they suffered on Dolphin Island – the rough seas threw up all sorts of useful objects.

He looked up and judged the position of the rising sun in the blue sky. *Maybe I'd better get back*, he thought.

But there was one more thing that grabbed his

attention, high on the beach, in amongst the bamboos. He strode towards it, trying to make out what it was, and only paused when a couple of cassowaries made a dash for it, out of the bamboo thicket and up on to the scrub-covered rocks. The flightless birds were smaller versions of emus, with the same strong legs for fast running but with blue necks and white heads.

Alfie waited until the cassowaries had reached safety then concentrated on the white thing flapping amongst the canes. At first he thought it was plastic, but then he saw that it was actually a large piece of canvas roughly two metres square, possibly from *Merlin* or from another boat that had come to grief during a storm. It was definitely part of a sail – tough and hard-wearing, stitched along two sides but torn away from something bigger still.

Mega find! was Alfie's first thought. He imagined what they could do with it. It could make a hammock, he decided, or an awning outside the shelter to shade them from the midday sun. He pulled the canvas free of the bamboos then folded it and rolled it into a tidy bundle, ready to hurry back with his latest trophy.

But then he had second thoughts – or not really a thought, more of an urge. Why not leave it here until he'd worked out the best use for it? If he took it back, Mia would pester him to make it into a new Supergirl cloak and the others would pitch in with their own ideas. He was the one who'd found it so he should be the one who decided. Much better to hide it somewhere and think about what to do with it.

So he chose a crevice in the rocks and tucked the bundle safely inside. Then he went to collect the rest of his stash and carry it back. 'Look what I found!' he announced to his mum and dad who were sitting by the fire eating breakfast. Fleur and Mia were already busy keeping a lookout from the mountain. 'This can, an old flip-flop and a plastic bag.'

Katie looked as if she was about to tell him off for going it alone, but James jumped in. 'Good work,' he told Alfie with a grin. 'Who said thirteen was an unlucky number?'

Alfie deposited his finds inside the shelter then re-emerged. 'Huh?'

'This is Day 13, remember?'

'Right. Cool.' Alfie tried to grin back and ignore his mum's frown. His stomach tied itself into a small knot and he felt uneasy. Why was she looking at him like that? She couldn't possibly know about the stashed-away piece of canvas, could she?

'Come and have breakfast,' Katie said quietly. 'Your dad's feeling a lot, lot better, by the way. He even reckons he could take a turn up at the lookout tomorrow if he continues to improve.'

Chapter Seven

'Where are you sneaking off to?' Fleur asked Alfie later that day. She and Mia had been for a swim after they'd got back from the lookout and as she waded out of the sea she saw him heading over the headland towards Turtle Beach.

'Nowhere,' he fibbed. He turned his gaze to the sea. 'I was just looking for Pearl.'

'They're not here,' Fleur reported. 'We'd have seen them from the lookout if they were heading this way.'

The reminder of the missing dolphins made Mia pout. 'Why aren't they here? Aren't they friends with us any more?'

'Hush,' Fleur told her. She thought Alfie was acting strangely for some reason. 'No, really – where were you going?'

He made up what he hoped was a good excuse. 'To find the other flip-flop – to match the one I found earlier.'

'No time now – supper's ready.' Fleur pointed up the beach to where their dad stood and waved. 'Anyway, you're supposed to tell people where you're going. It's a rule.'

'Yeah, yeah.' Reluctantly Alfie turned around and backtracked across the sand. He sat by the fire and ate in glum silence. Why couldn't Fleur leave him alone instead of poking her nose in all the time?

'What's wrong, Alfie?' James asked at the end of the meal.

'Nothing.' He glared at Fleur. 'Now can I go and look for the other flip-flop? Is that OK, Your Majesty?'

'Why are you having a go at me?' Fleur was stung into an angry reply. 'I only said you have to let people know where you're going. That's true, isn't it, Mum?'

'Alfie! Fleur!' His dad stepped in between them. 'No one's going anywhere until you've both said sorry.'

The apologies were uttered between gritted teeth but the bad feeling stayed. As James sat by the fire with Mia to tell her a story, Fleur wandered off down the beach while Alfie followed the path up the cliff. No one saw him go.

He climbed and then stopped by the waterfall to study the stretch of scrubland ahead. Over to the left, hidden by an overhang, was the ledge where they kept a lookout. His mum would be there, keeping the fire going as usual. Down below, Fleur paddled at the water's edge and James and Mia were hidden by smoke from the campfire.

OK, so the truth was that Alfie was hatching a plan. He hadn't been going to look for the flip-flop but no one needed to know that. Of course, the canvas that he'd stashed away would still be there tomorrow. For now he would take a different route up the mountain, leaving the waterfall and heading for an area they'd never explored before, staying out of sight of everyone below. The higher he went, scrambling from rock to rock and crawling through bushes, the further he would be able to see.

*

'Did you make up properly with Alfie?' James asked

Fleur as she headed back to camp. He'd been feeling well enough to stroll down the beach to meet her.

'It wasn't my fault,' she protested. 'It was Alfie's. He's been acting weird lately.'

'Yes.' Realizing she might be right, her dad looked thoughtful. 'He seems to have something on his mind. I wonder what it is.'

'Search me.' Fleur was tired and didn't want to talk. Instead, she breathed in the cool evening air and when they reached the shelter she went straight inside to join Mia.

James eased himself down on to a rocky ledge and enjoyed sitting in the open for a change. For the first time since they'd been shipwrecked, he was able to notice things other than the pain in his ribs – the bats flitting in and out of George's cave, for instance, and the gecko himself darting into their shelter where he would spend the night close to Fleur. Returning to camp, James saw that someone had done a good job of weighting down the cover of their food store with heavy rocks and that there was a supply of firewood to keep them going until morning.

‘Does anyone know where Alfie went?’ He leaned into the shelter to ask his question. ‘I haven’t seen him for a while.’

Typical Alfie, Fleur thought. *Once you tell him not to do something, he goes straight ahead and does it. Sometimes he doesn’t even know he’s doing it. That’s just the way he is – dreamy and in a world of his own.*

‘Maybe he went looking for the flip-flop,’ Mia suggested.

‘That’s not such a good idea right now – it’ll soon be dark.’ Their dad went back out and scanned the shoreline then the headlands. The sun was already touching the horizon, casting a pink glow across wispy white clouds. ‘Girls, can you go down to the rocks and take a look?’

Happy to help, Mia ran to one headland while Fleur took the other. They scanned the neighbouring bays without success. Meanwhile their dad cupped his hands around his mouth and yelled as loud as he could to Katie. ‘Is Alfie up there with you?’

He was too far away for Katie to hear but she saw

him signalling. 'What's up?' she yelled back. Her voice too was carried away on the wind.

'*Where is he?*' Frustrated and with a sense of rising panic, Fleur left the headland and ran back up the beach. Like Mia, she'd been guessing that Alfie had sneaked off to Turtle Beach again in search of the flip-flop but she'd looked carefully and the bay had been deserted. 'Alfie!' she muttered under her breath as she got close to camp. 'This isn't funny!'

'Alfie!' Mia's high voice echoed Fleur's. She joined Fleur and James with a trembling lip and tears in her eyes. 'He can't have gone away without telling us, can he?' she murmured.

'No – there's nowhere for him to go.' Fleur held her hand. 'Come with me – we'll climb the cliff together and find out if Mum knows where he is.'

Their dad agreed with this plan. 'Try not to worry – Alfie can't have gone far. But it's getting dark so be very careful.'

'Alfie!' Mia kept on calling his name as she and Fleur climbed the cliff out of deep shadows into the last rays of sunlight. 'Alfie, where are you?'

They dislodged loose stones and sent them rattling down the rock face, disturbing the cockatoos that roosted in the palm trees next to their camp. The white birds squawked crossly as they flew up into the sky.

'Rest for a minute – we're almost there.' Fleur paused by the waterfall and looked around. What if Alfie had wandered off and had an accident? There were hundreds of dangers out there – wild animals that they might not know about yet, a dark jungle to get lost in, steep rock faces to fall down or underwater currents that could easily sweep you out to sea. She shook her head to ward off this last, scariest thought. 'Come on,' she told Mia, 'we'd better see if Mum knows where he is.'

They were about to move on when Fleur noticed a movement high up the mountain. No – with a shrug of her shoulders, she told herself to ignore it – it was probably nothing.

'Come back, Alfie!' Mia's piping, frantic cry split the air. This time Katie heard her and set off from her ledge towards the waterfall to find out what was going on.

Fleur looked a second time at the expanse of scrubland covering the steep, unexplored slope. Now she was more certain – something was definitely moving amongst the bushes – perhaps a tree kangaroo searching for food before the sun went down, or the macaques setting out on a naughty night-time raid.

'Alfie!' a desperate Mia called.

He emerged suddenly from the bushes, leaning back on his heels as he made his descent, sending down a small avalanche of stones. He kept his arms wide for balance. 'What?' he yelled.

'We thought you'd got lost,' Fleur called back while Mia started to scramble up the slope to meet him. He tipped back his hat then crouched to listen to her while she talked excitedly and pointed towards Fleur and Katie. Then he nodded and they carried on down the slope together.

Katie took in the scene. 'What now?' she muttered to Fleur. 'Did he go walkabout without telling anyone?'

Beside herself with relief, Fleur could only nod.

'It's OK, he's here now.' Despite her soothing words, Katie's face had the determined, frowning look that

Fleur recognized.

'What?' Alfie repeated, all innocence as he and Mia hurried to the waterfall. He stared wide-eyed at Fleur and his mum, as if asking what all the fuss was about.

'Where've you been?' Fleur demanded. 'Didn't you hear us calling you?'

'Yes, he did.' Mia was overjoyed that they'd found him. She bubbled with mischievous excitement.

'Well then?' Hands on hips, Katie waited for an explanation.

'He was hiding from us on purpose,' Mia told them with a giggle.

'Oh, Alfie!' Fleur spread her palms in disgust.

Mia didn't get it. As far as she was concerned, everything was OK now. 'You were playing hide and seek, weren't you, Alfie?'

'Yeah, I was.' He glared at Fleur then set off ahead of the others with a *don't bug me* toss of his head.

*

'Hide and seek!' James echoed when they'd all gathered by the fire. Katie had left the lookout spot untended for once and caught up with Alfie then marched him down to camp. 'Are you serious?'

'Sorry,' Alfie grunted. He stood in the centre of the group, hanging his head.

Hide and seek? Fleur felt so angry with him that she thought she would burst. All that fuss and worry for nothing.

'Never, ever go off by yourself again,' Katie insisted. 'It's not safe and it's not fair on the rest of us to make us wonder where you've got to.'

'OK, I won't,' he promised, shamefaced.

'Good. Now let's all take a deep breath and count to ten,' James suggested. 'The crisis is over. It's high time to get some sleep.'

*

Alfie lay awake as usual while his dad, Mia and Fleur slept. Katie was high on the mountain, keeping watch.

If only they knew what I know! He hugged his secret to him, running through what he'd discovered from his new vantage point. There was an island – an actual *island* – on the horizon that nobody else had spotted. It was hazy and faint and he didn't know how big it was or what it was called, only that it was there.

Lying in the dark, he thought up a name – Misty Island!

So what if there's an island? The worm of doubt inside his head challenged him as he lay in the dark. *What difference does it make?*

It was obvious, wasn't it? Alfie stared out at the moon and stars. I could go there on the raft and find out if anyone lives there, he told his inner voice.

You're crazy. It's too far away to row there, you dummy!

Who said anything about rowing, *dummy*?

How else are you going to get there?

I can make a sail, can't I? Hah – you didn't expect that! I've got something to make a sail with, stashed away where no one can find it. I can soon build a mast without anybody knowing and fix the sail to it with lianas and rope. Then I'll sail there on the raft. Now who's calling who a dummy?

The voice of doubt retreated for a while then wriggled back out of the dark corners of Alfie's mind. *Fleur would try to stop you*, it said.

She won't find out. Tomorrow I'll sneak off to make the sail. Fleur won't see me.

Yes, she will. You know what she's like – she'll never let you get away with it. Anyway, what's the point? There probably won't be anyone there on that island, even if you do get that far.

Alfie rolled on to his side and stared out to sea. Bright moonlight turned the restless waves silver. How can I know if I don't try? He pictured the bamboo raft after he'd finished working on it. It would have the four containers for buoyancy, plus a mast and a jib made out of driftwood and a new canvas sail. He would take the oars to steer with. That's how people had sailed before boats had engines, using the wind to get where they wanted to go. I can do this! he told himself. I can sail to the next island and fetch help.

Really? the doubting inner voice said in disbelief. *Aren't you forgetting something?*

What? Angry and still wide awake, Alfie crawled out of the shelter and sat cross-legged by the fire. All he could think of was sailing to the island and being a hero.

You and the sea.

What about me and the sea?

You can't stand it. It gives you nightmares.

Ah yes, in the excitement of making his secret plan, this is what Alfie had overlooked. He stared into the fire, trying to block out the knowledge. As burning logs shifted and sank down, red sparks danced upwards. 'It'll be OK,' he said out loud.

The voice didn't argue back. His thoughts grew settled. Tomorrow was Day 14 and he would spend it working on the raft. At first light on Day 15 he would set sail for the island and save his family.

Chapter Eight

'Monkey, where are you?'

The search was on for Mia's favourite toy. Had she left him in George's cave? Fleur wondered. Or was he tucked away under the bushes outside the shelter?

Mia had missed him the moment she woke up, and Alfie and Fleur had searched everywhere while James had sliced up fruit for breakfast.

'Monkey!' Mia called out his name as if he could really hear her. 'This isn't funny!'

'Here he is.' Alfie went into the shelter and saw a flattened, furry tail sticking out from underneath Mia's sleeping mat. 'He was here all the time.'

'Wow – thanks, Alfie. Bad Monkey!' Mia took him and gave him a shake.

'Now can we get on and collect firewood?' Fleur

wanted to know as she gobbled down some jackfruit.

'You do that. I'll take the raft and go crabbing.' Alfie spoke with his mouth full and hastily left camp before his dad had a chance to object. He heard James say to Fleur that he felt well enough to make his first climb up to the lookout point later in the day and listened to Fleur telling their dad he should carry on resting until he'd finished taking the antibiotics. Letting them argue it out and leaving Mia to carry on scolding Monkey, Alfie hurried to the raft and began to drag it down to the water's edge. The sky was clear and there was no wind – ideal conditions for what he had in mind.

Mia saw him and followed him. 'Can I come crabbing too?' she wheedled.

'No.' Alfie's answer was short and not very sweet.

Disappointed, she trotted ahead then stood in his path. 'Why not?'

''Cos ...'cos ... just because!' Alfie frowned angrily.

Luckily James chose this moment to call Mia back. 'I need you to take a message to Mum. Climb up the cliff and tell her I'm feeling a lot better today. Say she can come down for breakfast. I'll definitely swap with her and take my turn at the lookout.'

This left Alfie free to carry on dragging the raft to the shore where he hopped on, waited for it to steady itself then used the paddles to row quickly around the headland towards Turtle Beach.

Back at camp, Fleur added two planks of driftwood to the pile of logs and branches for the fire. She'd discovered them in George's cave, along with a blue flip-flop that matched the one Alfie had found. 'Cool – now we've got a pair,' she'd murmured as she'd picked it up. They looked the right size for Katie and though they were bashed and had little chunks of rubber missing, Fleur reckoned they would still come in handy.

'Can I take these up to Mum?' she asked James, who was inside the shelter rolling up the sleeping mats. She'd picked up the other flip-flop from a ledge by the door and held them up to show him.

'Sure – good idea. Take a couple of water bottles with you and fill them up on your way back down.' Two weeks on Dolphin Island had given the kids' dad a thick, dark beard and a deep tan, so that he looked strong and healthy in spite of his injured ribs. 'Remember – tell Mum I'm ready to take my turn up there later today.'

So Fleur set off up the cliff with an empty bottle in either hand and with one flip-flop sticking out of each back pocket, eager to see if they fitted her mum. When she reached the waterfall, she wedged the bottles between some stones, ready for later, took a quick look out to sea (no dolphins) then hurried on up.

'Flip-flops!' she announced as she approached Katie and Mia at the lookout, drawing the salvaged footwear out of her back pockets.

Katie gave a whoop of delight, sounding for a second more like a kid than a grown-up. Eagerly she took off her trainers and tried them on then wiggled her toes. 'Luxury – pure luxury,' she sighed.

'Dad says he wants to take a turn—'

'I know,' Katie interrupted, back to her usual down-to-earth tone. 'Mia told me. That's your crazy dad for you – he always tries to do too much. You two stay here – I'm going to go and tell him it's still too soon.'

This left Mia and Fleur perched like eagles on the

mountain ledge, keeping the fire going and searching the horizon for shipping.

'Come on, ships, why don't you sail this way?' Fleur wondered out loud. She raised her hand to shade her eyes and carried on looking. 'Cruise liners, oil-tankers, container ships, family yachts – anything!'

After a while Mia grew bored and began to pick up shiny, flat rocks that she built into a tower – higher and higher until it toppled then she would begin all over again.

Meanwhile, Fleur's eyes grew strained from looking out to sea and when she closed them she almost dozed off. She jolted awake and tried to concentrate again.

'Watch!' Mia said. Her tower grew taller. She held her breath and added two more stones.

'It's wobbling,' Fleur warned. 'Look out …'

Mia balanced a final stone on the top then they both groaned as it collapsed. With a sigh Mia turned to look down into their bay criss-crossed with their footprints and she seemed suddenly unhappy. 'It's not fair – Alfie wouldn't let me go crabbing with him.'

'Hmm, never mind.' Fleur was distracted by a

change for the worse in the weather. A wind had got up, blowing smoke from the fire in their direction. It stung her eyes and made her cough but when she took Mia to the far side of the ledge, out of its range, the wind suddenly changed direction and blew in their faces again.

'Yuck!' Mia breathed in the smoke. Her eyes watered.

'It's OK – you go down,' Fleur decided, pointing to the clouds gathering out to sea. 'Take a message – tell Mum and Dad we might be in for another storm, worse luck.'

'Not again,' Mia moaned.

'Yes, again,' Fleur said as she scanned the horizon. Right now the clouds looked fluffy and harmless in the sunlight but they would soon turn dark and bring rain. That's how it was in the tropics – a sunny paradise of palm trees, white sands and blue sea one minute, the next a whirling, rain-lashed hell.

*

All morning Alfie worked to make a mast and a jib. After he'd rounded the headland on to Turtle Beach and disappeared from sight, he'd dragged the raft out of the sea and fifty metres up the beach until it was hidden amongst the thicket of bamboos. Would one of the canes work as a mast? he wondered.

He experimented but soon found that bamboo was too bendy. He needed something sturdier and this meant scouring the bay for a straight branch or piece of driftwood that he could strip and whittle into shape with the knife he'd brought from the shelter. He searched under bushes and rocks, checking that his piece of sailcloth was still safely wedged in its crevice, until at last he found what he was looking for – two lengths of wood that he could lash together in the shape of a cross.

This is taking ages, he sighed to himself after he'd carried the wood back to his hiding place and noticed that the sun was already high. *If I want to get this finished without anyone noticing, I have to work faster!*

The next job was to fix the mast to the middle of the raft, but again this took longer than Alfie expected because he had to carve a hole in the platform with his knife and the hole had to be exactly the right size. In the end he managed it, jammed the mast tight into the hole then stood back again to examine his progress.

It was then that he felt the first spot of rain. He looked out from the stand of bamboos at dark clouds rolling in from the sea then felt more cold splashes on his face.

Brilliant! Alfie suddenly realized that for once the bad weather was actually on his side.

It gave him the chance to leave the raft safely hidden in the bamboo thicket then sprint down the beach. By the time he reached the headland, a strong wind was driving the waves high on to the rocks and rain stung his arms and legs. He had to lean into it and keep his head down, leaping over rock pools, almost blinded by spray. He made it to the far side and carried on running towards camp.

From her eagle's eyrie high on the mountain, Fleur saw Alfie's small figure appear on the rocks. He battled the wind and rain, vanished in sea spray then emerged, head down, still fighting the storm. She watched him run up the beach.

Where's the raft? she wondered. A knot formed in her stomach and she had a tingling feeling that something bad had happened.

'Emergency!' Alfie yelled as he drew near the shelter.

James, Katie and Mia came to the doorway. Smoke from the fire formed a screen between them and Alfie.

Mia darted out to meet him. 'Alfie, what's wrong?'

His hair was plastered to his skull, his T-shirt and shorts drenched. 'Where's Dad?'

'In here with Mum,' James called. 'Come inside out of the rain.'

Mia led the way, dragging Alfie after her. He shivered then shook raindrops from his head.

'Are you all right?' Katie checked. As long as everyone was safe, nothing else really mattered.

'I'm OK, I'm OK.' He bent double, hands on knees, trying to catch his breath.

'Didn't we say for you not to go off without telling us?' James reminded him.

'I didn't. I said I was going crabbing – remember?' This was the alibi that Alfie had put in place, hoping that it would keep him out of trouble. 'The raft ... the storm,' he gasped.

Katie cast a worried look at James. Outside the shelter, the fire hissed in the pelting rain. Steam mingled with smoke and threatened to kill the flames. 'Exactly what happened?' she asked Alfie.

'I left the raft by the rocks on Turtle Beach and went to catch crabs,' he gabbled. This was where good luck and the bad weather had been on Alfie's side. 'It ... it floated away in the storm,' he added with a helpless shrug.

'"Floated away"?' Mia echoed.

'You mean the wind and the currents carried it away?' James asked with a sinking heart.

Alfie nodded. He felt his stomach churn and his mouth go dry because this was the biggest lie he'd told in his whole life.

'The current dragged it out to sea?' Katie shook her head in dismay.

'Yes. The waves were too high – I couldn't stop it,' he said miserably.

Katie and James gazed outside at a sheet of rain and

listened to the roar of wind and waves. For a while no one said anything as they realized what the loss of the raft might mean.

'It's OK, you did the right thing,' James said eventually. 'I'm glad you didn't try to wade into the sea after it. We'd much rather have you safely back in one piece.'

'Yes,' Alfie's mum agreed. 'We can build a new raft. There's only one of you, Alfie Fisher. And there's no way we could find another.'

*

Sometimes you had to do the wrong thing for the right reasons, Alfie told himself. The lie weighed heavily on his shoulders so he did his best to worm out from under its shadow.

By mid-afternoon the storm had passed and the sea was calm and blue again. Katie was back at the lookout, James was resting in the shelter, doing as Katie had instructed, and Alfie, Fleur and Mia were at the water's edge watching a shoal of silversides swim in the shallows. The tiny fish glinted in the sunlight as they darted in and out of sea grass uprooted by the latest storm.

'Yuck! Jellyfish alert!' Mia cried as she hopped over one of the transparent stinging creatures stranded on the shoreline. Then she plunged deeper into the water and began to swim.

Telling the big lie about the raft had left Alfie feeling wretched and unsure, but it was only the start of his secret mission, before he put the main plan into action. Just wait until he sailed off to the new island, he told himself. He would land there and find people with boats. They would have medicines, phones and compasses, charts and radar – all the things that he, Alfie Fisher, needed to rescue his family from Dolphin Island.

Imagine how cool that will feel, he told himself as Fleur waded into the sea to join Mia. *Don't think about the bad parts.*

Fleur took a deep breath then threw herself forward and dived underwater. She kicked hard and came up again ten metres from the shore then swam breaststroke beside Mia for a little while. 'What exactly did Alfie say about the raft?' she asked.

'When?' Mia said before she did a quick underwater

somersault. She came up again holding her nose and with her hair streaming over her face.

'Earlier – when I was keeping lookout.'

'He said it floated away.'

'How come?' Fleur had only heard a quick version of the story from their mum when Katie had come up to the lookout to take over. Now she wanted to hear it again from Mia.

'Dunno.' Mia sculled with her hands and rolled on the surface. 'Watch – I'm a dolphin!'

'Floated away – how?' Fleur insisted. Surely Alfie would have seen the storm coming and had time to make sure that the raft was safe by lugging it higher on to the beach. Then again, they all knew he'd been acting funny lately. Besides, he was never that practical at the best of times. It was her, Fleur, who was the sensible one. 'You take after me,' her mum would tell her. 'We both like making lists and studying nature. Alfie and Mia – they're the dreamers.'

'Like Dad?' Fleur had asked.

'Your dad is a mixture – part dreamer, part handyman.' Katie had chuckled her reply. 'Together the Fisher family makes a pretty good team.'

'Alfie said the raft floated away in the middle of the storm,' Mia told Fleur now as she drifted on her back and let her hair drift on the surface. She'd switched from dolphin to mermaid. 'Mum wants us to build another one, starting tomorrow.'

Lazily Fleur and Mia swam breaststroke in slow circles while Alfie stayed on the shore and watched out for dolphins.

'That means we'll have to fetch loads more bamboo from Turtle Beach,' Fleur realized.

'And more floaty canister thingies,' Mia added.

'If we can find any.'

'And fetch more creepers from the jungle to tie everything together with.' It was hard work and both girls knew it.

'Yes, we'll have to build another platform, starting all over again,' Fleur said with a weary sigh.

Chapter Nine

Alfie still had lots of work to do on the raft. He made himself stay awake by thinking how he would fix the sail to the mast using rope salvaged from the shore and creepers from the jungle. He worked it out carefully then listened to George's tiny feet scampering over the shelter floor. He watched the gecko settle on a ledge close to Fleur then listened again. There was more movement – this time outside the shelter. So he crept out into the open without waking the others to find three macaques tugging at the covering to their food store. He could see them clearly in the moonlight. 'Shoo!' he hissed, waving his arms at them.

The monkeys spied Alfie and sped away into the bushes then straight up the palm tree trunks and out of sight.

Surprised by how light it was under the moon and stars, and with his head stuffed full of his secret plan, Alfie decided on the spur of the moment that now was the time to set off for Turtle Beach. After all, why wait for the sun to rise?

So, with bated breath, he collected all the rope and creepers he could carry and took the knife from its ledge. He moved silently and when he was ready, he took one last look inside the shelter. Mia lay snuggled up with Monkey and George stood guard over Fleur. James was fast asleep in his hammock.

'Don't worry, I won't be long.' Holding his breath, Alfie whispered a promise before he left. Then he crept away, along the beach and on to the headland, over the rocks on to Turtle Beach.

Gaining courage from the strength of the moonlight, he jumped down on to the sand then strode on, only stopping to remove the hidden canvas from its crevice in the rocks. Then he headed for the stand of bamboos and laid the canvas flat on the sand. He cut it into a rough triangle and pierced holes down two sides, quickly threading rope through the holes before tying the canvas to the mast and jib. Then he stood back to examine his work. Cool – the sail was starting to look the way he wanted.

It had been a good idea to leave camp early, he decided – with luck, the work would be finished by dawn and he could set off for Misty Island before any of the others were awake.

Alfie glanced out to sea – there was a clear sky and hardly any wind. The water glittered with silvery light. *Don't be scared – you can do this!* he thought. *All you have to do is be brave and follow the plan!*

At last, with the canvas securely tied in place, he laid the finished mast and sail flat on the raft and lugged the whole thing down the beach, leaving a wide groove in the sand. When he reached the shore he raised the mast and jammed it in place then he shoved the raft into the water. A light wind flapped at the sail and the raft jerked forward out of reach. Yes – his idea would definitely work! Making sure that the oars were close at hand, he splashed into the waves and jumped on board, getting his balance before grabbing the oars and using them like a rudder to steer straight out to sea. His heart was in his mouth, his mouth felt dry, but his plan was working!

Under the moon and stars, Alfie felt the light wind fill his sail and propel him forward, away from Dolphin Island.

*

Back in the shelter, Fleur woke up. The moon still shone. She heard the comforting crackle of the fire outside and in its low, flickering light she turned over, ready to go back to sleep.

But then she noticed that Alfie was missing from his sleeping mat and she sat up suddenly. *What now?* she wondered. She felt the familiar knot in her stomach and an urge to crawl outside and find him. Luckily the moon was full and there was plenty of light. *Where is he? What's he up to?*

She searched hard but couldn't see him by the fire or down by the shore – except for herself and Mia and James sleeping in the shelter, the bay was deserted. OK, so maybe Alfie had taken it into his head to climb the cliff to join their mum at the lookout. Yes – that must be it. Taking a deep breath and trying to settle her fears, Fleur was about to go back into the shelter. She took one last look at the sea – so beautiful and calm, reflecting the light from the moon. Then she gazed out beyond the rocks where *Merlin* had sunk, far out towards the horizon. *Wait!* There were three dolphins close to *Merlin*'s rock, swimming purposefully towards the shore.

They came swiftly towards her, their fins visible above the smooth water. Without stopping to think, Fleur ran down the beach and into the sea. Soon she was close enough to recognize Jazz and then Pearl and Stormy, who circled her before swimming straight towards the Turtle Beach headland and back again. They slapped their tail flukes against the surface and clicked and chattered urgently.

OK, I get it! Fleur realized that the dolphins wanted her to climb on to the headland. They kept a close watch as she headed towards the rocks and clambered over them into the neighbouring bay. *This is about Alfie*, she thought with a growing sense of dread. *He's done something stupid – I know it!*

From the headland she scanned the small, empty

beach. She made out a wide groove in the sand, leading from the bamboos down to the water's edge. Although at first she couldn't work out what had made the marks, her heart twisted with fear.

Jazz and Stormy swam close to the rocks, raising their heads out of the water to click and whistle. They flicked their tail and their dark eyes glittered in the moonlight. Meanwhile Pearl surged out to sea and then back again, impatiently back and forth until at last she swam further out and waited.

Fleur watched Pearl cut through the water. She raised her eyes towards the horizon, following Pearl's course across the sea, and felt shock run through her from top to toe. There, already quite far out, was a white sail mounted on a raft. There was somebody on board – a small, solitary figure in blue shorts and a striped T-shirt struggling to keep control of his flimsy craft.

'Oh no – Alfie!' Fleur groaned. She raised her voice and cupped her hands to her mouth to call after him. 'Alfie, come back!'

He didn't hear. Further out to sea, the wind started

to gather strength. It caught the sail and drove the raft further from land. Waves tipped it violently forward and back, forcing Alfie to cling on to the mast. Then, without warning, the wind changed direction and the sail swung round. As he ducked under the swinging jib, he lost his hold on the oars and they slipped from the raft into the sea. He reached out and made a frantic grab for them – too late, they were gone. Without them, he couldn't steer. Now his best hope was to hang on to the mast and pray that the wind would carry him to safety.

'Oh no,' Fleur groaned again. She watched Stormy and Jazz head out after Pearl and Alfie, plunging below the waves as they gathered speed. Sick to her stomach, she turned and scrambled over the rocks then struggled through the soft white sand towards the shelter. Katie's fire burned high up the mountain, the nearby campfire flickered gently. 'Dad, wake up!' she cried.

Mia and James woke to the sound of her urgent voice. They rushed out of the shelter.

'Alfie's gone!' Fleur cried, wild-eyed and incoherent with fear.

'Gone where?' Still half asleep, James was confused.

She collapsed, sobbing, into his arms. 'Dad, I saw him. He went out on the raft.'

'How could he? Alfie said the raft was swept away in the storm.'

'No, it turns out that wasn't true. He must have hidden it and lied to us. Now he's taken it out to sea. Come quickly, you have to see this!'

*

The flimsy raft bobbed up and down. Alfie hung on tight as it crested wave after wave then plunged down again. His arms started to ache and his wet fingers grew numb with cold. How much longer could he hold on?

As for the sail, it flapped loudly between strong gusts as the wind pushed the raft this way and that. Alfie was swept along at the mercy of the currents, without control and with fear gripping his heart.

Up went the raft, tilting him backwards. It reached the crest of the wave and held him still for a moment, left him poised for a sickening second before plunging down and thrusting him forward, choking him with

panic. As he dropped, he was certain that this time the raft would disappear underwater, taking him with it. He would lose hold of the mast and a wave would snatch him. A current would drag him down, down, down …

Overhead, the moon and stars whirled. The sail flapped harder than ever; the mast creaked and bowed under the strain.

*

James and Mia ran with Fleur over the headland on to Turtle Beach. They were in time to see Alfie's raft pulled further and further away from land, bobbing on the waves like a cork.

'See!' Fleur cried in horror.

Mia spotted the tiny craft and straight away started to sob.

James took a deep, shuddering breath. 'What on earth was he thinking?'

The faintest glimmer of light appeared in the east and the stars started to fade from the sky. Still the ocean current drew the raft further from land out to sea.

Mia said what they all felt. 'Alfie's lost,' she

whimpered. 'He's never coming back.'

*

His worst nightmare had come true. The sea had him in its grip and would not let him go. Waves towered over him then broke in furious white foam, battering him with their brute force. Currents swept him along to who knew what danger – to rocks and reefs, over hidden tiny islands lying just below the surface or out into the wide, wide ocean.

He, Alfie Fisher, had to hang on to the mast with every last scrap of strength and crest every wave. He must not lose hold and plunge into the cold, cruel depths, down with the hungry snappers, the ugly, gaping groupers and stinging jellyfish, the treacherous tangles of sea grass and coral.

Dawn came. A flat grey light crept over the horizon, followed by a blood-red sun that rose slowly over the ocean. Alfie clung to the creaking mast, all thoughts of reaching his secret island long gone.

All he could do as day came was to cling on. Cling on and wait.

Chapter Ten

The sun rose in a cloudless sky. From the raft all Alfie could see was water, but thank goodness the wind had died down and the sea was calmer, giving him a chance to get his bearings. East was where the sun appeared, so at this point Dolphin Island must be behind him. To the south, hundreds of miles away, was the coast of Australia. To the north were the thousands of small islands that made up Micronesia.

He frowned and sat hunched on the rocking, lurching platform, still holding on to the mast for safety. *What had been the point of taking time to work that out*, he wondered with a deep sigh. *Even in calm water, the currents are pushing me south and they're too strong for me to fight against – I just have to go where they take me.*

But then a new current turned him north and a fresh, warm breeze set in, billowing out the sail and carrying him rapidly in the direction of the southern tip of Dolphin Island. *Yes!* he said to himself. *Take me back to where I started from – please!*

Buffeted by choppy waves, Alfie strained to see the mountain that towered over the island he called home, not noticing yet another abrupt change in the wind or the strong tow of a fresh current. It was only when he heard the loud crash of waves against rock that he turned to see that he was sailing close to four jagged, dark spikes and managed just in time to swing the sail around and gather enough wind to skirt around the danger.

As he cleared the rocks, he leaned forward and groaned, trying to block out the thought of what would have happened if he'd not seen them in time. A picture flashed into his mind of the mast splitting in two and the bamboo platform shattering to pieces, of him losing his balance and being thrown into the relentless waves and all-powerful undertow. He shuddered. It was no good – his narrow escape had left him more terrified than ever.

On he went through the morning, grasping the mast with one hand and trying to shield his eyes from the glare of the sun with the other. The waves rocked him and the heat made his mouth feel dry so he cooled himself by dipping his free hand into the sea and sprinkling his shoulders with salt water which dried on his T-shirt almost instantly.

He squinted into the sun and judged that the wind and currents had been carrying him steadily north for quite a while now. Surely, if he looked hard enough, he would soon see the longed for coast of Dolphin Island. He stared and stared, picturing the jungle slopes with their thick, shadowy covering of trees, thinking that he did see them and jumping to his feet in excitement until the imagined, hazy mountain faded from his vision and he realized that what he'd been looking at was a cruel mirage. Worse still, he realized that the wind had changed again and was carrying him south, back into the wide ocean.

Alfie's cry of despair was drowned out by the sound of waves lapping against the raft. He hung his head and closed his eyes. When he opened them again and gazed down into the turquoise water, he made out the sleek grey shape of a dolphin rising to the surface.

No – it couldn't be! This was another mirage, a figment of his imagination.

But Pearl rose up from the clear depths. Her snout broke the surface, soon followed by the dome of her head and her dorsal fin then the whole length of her smooth, shining body. She greeted Alfie with her cheerful, chirping whistle.

'Pearl, is it you?' He could hardly believe it. He wasn't alone on the ocean after all.

She rolled easily on to her side, showing him her beautiful pearly pink belly, then lightly rested a flipper on the side of the raft.

Alfie felt it tilt towards her. He reached out to touch her velvety flank. 'It is!' he said with a sob of relief. 'Oh, you found me – thank you, thank you!'

Pearl slapped her tail flukes against the water. Her upturned mouth seemed to smile at him.

Alfie's shift of weight as he held his arms out towards her made the raft rock dangerously and he had to lean backwards to stop himself from sliding into the water.

As he grabbed the mast to regain his balance, a strong gust of wind caught the sail and sent him skimming away from Pearl, who followed at a safe distance, waiting for the raft to right itself.

The wind tore at the sail and strained at its rope ties. The raft lurched forward then sideways. Alfie gasped as it gathered speed. He saw the knots that held the sail in place start to unravel, one after another, so that the canvas tore loose from the mast. It fell on to him, trapping him beneath. He clawed at it and dragged himself clear – only to see the limp sail slide over the edge of the platform and bend the mast under its sodden weight. There was a sharp crack as the top of the mast broke away.

Desperate to save the waterlogged sail, Alfie lay on his belly and did his best to haul it back on board. It was too heavy and the current was dragging it away, pulling it down out of sight.

Helplessly Alfie let go and watched it sink then turned to Pearl for help. 'What now?' he begged. With a flick of her tail she swam close and started to nudge the raft with her snout, pushing him steadily against the current. He didn't know why she wanted to guide him in this direction, but he trusted her. So he sat on the bare platform, gripping on to what was left of the mast, staring ahead at waves breaking against some low, dark rocks.

Alfie's heart was in his mouth but Pearl pushed hard, using the strength of her tail to propel them through the water. Soon they were close enough to the rocks for Alfie to feel the spray from the breaking waves. He made out that they were approaching a coral reef that formed an almost complete circle with a narrow entrance into a blue lagoon where the water seemed shallower and less choppy. This sheltered place was where they were headed, thanks to clever, confident Pearl who steered him through the gap.

This is called an atoll, Alfie realized. He'd seen them before – circular coral reefs that rose only a few metres clear of the water. Sometimes the lagoons within the circle were wide – as much as twenty kilometres across – but this was small – maybe half a kilometre in width and fringed with sand. As he looked down into the vivid turquoise water, he saw that the water was shallow – perhaps two metres or so – with stingrays gliding close to the bottom and brightly coloured angelfish and damselfish darting here and there.

As Pearl stopped pushing and allowed the raft to drift, Alfie had time to take in his new surroundings. The dark red rocks were completely bare. There was no vegetation on the atoll but lots of debris dumped on the shore. He spotted driftwood and rusty oilcans tangled up with seaweed, bright white pieces of polystyrene foam, a tattered sheet of blue plastic big enough for him to build a shelter once he'd made it on to dry land. He pointed to the beach so that Pearl understood where he wanted to go then he lay on his belly and paddled the raft with his hands.

Pearl helped again by nudging with her snout. Soon Alfie felt the bottom of the raft scrape against sand and come to a juddering halt. He sprang up and jumped off the platform, overjoyed to feel firm ground under his feet. 'Thank you!' he cried. 'I don't have a clue where I am and I don't care. All I know is that I never want to sail a raft, ever again!'

*

James, Fleur and Mia stood on the headland and watched Alfie's raft disappear from view.

Fleur's stomach felt hollow; she could feel the thud of her heart against her ribs. 'I don't get it!'

'Me neither.' James let out a groaning sigh. 'I can't think what got into him.'

'Alfie, come back,' Mia whimpered.

Time seemed to stop and they stood for what felt like an age as the sun rose.

'Turn around, Alfie,' Fleur pleaded.

'Perhaps he can't,' James said through gritted teeth. He knew that it depended which way the wind was blowing and whether or not the raft was built strongly enough to survive the waves. 'Why did he have to make a sail and set off without us in the first place – that's what I don't understand.'

'He must have had a reason.' Fleur's thoughts flew back to the time two days earlier when Alfie had done his vanishing trick and they'd had to search for him. That had been the start of it, she decided. Alfie had laughed it off as a game of hide and seek, but really he must have climbed the mountain for a different reason, she realized now. He'd been quiet and moody afterwards and then he'd snuck off to go crabbing by himself on Turtle Beach and come home without the raft and with no crabs either.

Fleur tried her best to think like Alfie and put herself in his shoes. He was the one who couldn't forget about the shipwreck. She suspected he had bad dreams about the storm that he mostly kept to himself, but they made him scared to go into the sea and swim, even with the dolphins. Yet he was also the one out of all of them who was the most homesick and desperate to be rescued. 'What if he saw something – another island – from the top of the mountain then decided to set off to fetch help?' she asked, her heart thumping. 'That would be just like Alfie.'

James shuddered. 'He'll never make it on that raft. It isn't sturdy enough.'

Searching the horizon in vain, fear held them in its grip. 'Who's going to go up to the lookout and tell Mum?' Fleur whispered.

'No need – she's here.' Mia tugged at Fleur's hand

and pointed over her shoulder.

James and Fleur turned to see Katie run across the beach. She arrived gasping for breath. 'Did I just see Alfie leaving Turtle Beach on the raft?'

Too choked to speak, James simply nodded.

Katie turned to Fleur. 'Say it's not true!' she begged. Her throat made short, dry, rasping sounds as she tried to suck air into her lungs.

'It is – he sailed away.'

A last glimmer of hope faded from Katie's face and she sank to her knees. 'Mum, what are we going to do?' Fleur tried to raise her up but she needed help from her dad. Together they lifted her back on to her feet.

Katie shook her head. 'The tide, the currents,' she mumbled.

The words seemed to bring James to his senses. 'Exactly. The tide will soon turn. There's a chance that the raft will be pushed back onshore. One of us should set off and look.'

'Let me – I'll do that.' Katie decided to follow the coastline down to its southern tip. Even though the raft and Alfie had vanished over the horizon, she couldn't stand around doing nothing – she had to act.

'I'll climb the mountain and keep a lookout.' Though his ribs still hurt when he put his body under strain, James too was determined to play his part.

'What about me?' Mia pleaded.

'Come with me.' Following their mum and dad's example, Fleur leaped into action. As Katie set off on her search of the coast and James headed towards the cliff, she climbed the headland and started to run up Turtle Beach towards the stand of bamboos. 'The best thing to do is make a new raft,' she decided. 'We have to follow Alfie and bring him back safe even if it means working all day and all night.'

Chapter Eleven

It only took ten minutes for Alfie to explore his atoll. As Pearl watched from the calm, clear water of the lagoon, he dragged his battered raft on to the beach then climbed on to the coral reef and picked his way carefully over rough rocks. Already desperately thirsty, he followed the curve of the islet from one end to the other, picking up objects that might come in useful – a rusty can, a plastic sack and a punctured Spiderman football. He carried them under a fierce sun that dazzled him and scorched his arms and legs.

Before anything else, I need to make a shelter. Alfie remembered that this had been the family's first task when they'd arrived on Dolphin Island and so he put into action the skills he'd learned then. He took the plastic sack to the highest point of the atoll and chose a cleft between two rocks, stretching the sack across it to form a temporary roof that he fixed in place with loose rocks. Then he crept under its shade and gazed out to sea.

A few metres from the shore, Pearl kept watch. She seemed calm and gave no sign that she had plans to swim away and join her pod, sculling gently with her flippers and now and then giving an encouraging slap of her tail flukes against the water.

Thank you! Alfie gave her a grateful wave. As long as Pearl stayed with him, he could keep his fear at bay. Huddled under the plastic roof, he did his best to ignore his parched lips and bone-dry mouth, taking a deep breath and trying to work out a plan. He would have to shelter here for a few hours, resting and conserving his energy until it grew cooler. Then, as the sun went down he would be able to trawl the atoll for more useful stuff which he would bring back to his new base. As yet he had no idea what that would be or how he would use it, but for the time being all he could do was stay out of the sun, hugging his knees to his chest, watching Pearl circle around the dimpled surface of the lagoon and listening to the gentle waves lap against the reef.

*

On Dolphin Island, Katie hiked to the furthest tip, desperately searching every inlet for a sign that Alfie had managed to steer the raft ashore. She climbed rocks and waded through rock pools, crossed scorching beaches and peered into dark caves, all the time praying that the turning tide would bring her son safely back.

What was he thinking? Why did he break the rules? she asked herself over and over. Then her mood changed and she plunged from anger into despair. *I'm his mother – I should have noticed he was up to something. Why didn't I keep a closer eye on him and give him a chance to talk things through?*

Weighed down by guilt, she went on, clambering over the thick, tangled roots of a small mangrove swamp and ducking under low branches. She emerged, covered in mud and sweat, on to yet another headland, searching on until she came to a narrow cove on the very tip of the island.

Weary and desperate, she crouched to peer under shadowy ledges. She entered caves washed by the waves, calling Alfie's name. All she heard was the faint echo of her own voice, then silence.

*

On the cliff behind the shelter, James had to stop many times to catch his breath. It was hard to get air into his lungs without feeling a pain shoot through his chest but he carried on past the waterfall, up the mountain slope where Alfie had gone exploring.

If I find out exactly what Alfie saw from up there, then maybe I can work out the direction he planned to take, James decided. Wincing with every step, he bent his head and walked on across the scrubland, climbing higher until he reached the edge of the jungle then stopping to look out to sea.

The water was a deep azure blue, reflecting the colour of the sky. A heat haze made the horizon shimmer and dance. James narrowed his eyes and looked harder. Was that an island he could see off the southern tip of Dolphin Island, or was it a trick played by the heat haze? And, more interesting still, were there small atolls out there – dark reefs rising out of the water as the tide went out? James struggled to bring things into focus. Yes, he decided – there was a chain of tiny islets stretching into the ocean in the direction of the bigger island that shimmered in the distance. That's where Alfie was headed, he thought. Fleur was right. The crazy kid sailed off to fetch help without telling anyone. Typical Alfie. He knew how dangerous it might be but he went ahead and did it anyway.

*

On Turtle Beach, Fleur hacked at bamboo canes growing in the stand at the edge of the beach and laid them flat on the sand. Mia stripped the leaves from the tops. They worked without resting, using knives that they'd fetched from camp. At midday the heat of the sun forced them to stop.

'Let's go back to base for some rope and a drink of water.' Fleur decided they should take a break. 'Dad might be home by now – we'll ask him to help us make the platform.'

So she and Mia hurried over the headland, to be

met by their dad at the door to their shelter.

'You were right, Fleur – there is another island out there. And dozens of atolls.' Trying to reassure them, he made it sound as if this was a good thing. 'They're all places Alfie could have landed if need be.'

'You mean, if he didn't make it all the way to the new island?' Fleur wiped her forehead with the back of her hand. 'But what would happen then? He still can't get back home, can he?'

'Maybe, maybe not.' James was vague about how the currents would work. 'It would all depend.'

'But let's face it – the raft probably got wrecked and now he's stranded.' If this was true, Fleur tried to figure out how Alfie would cope. 'Say he did land on one of those atolls. There won't be anything to eat. And there's no water.'

'That's true,' her dad agreed slowly.

Picturing the lonely scene, Mia began to cry quietly.

'And say his raft *was* wrecked when he landed ...' Fleur's thoughts ran on. She knew how strong the tidal currents were and how scared Alfie was bound to be. 'He won't be able to get off again – he'll be stuck there.'

'We can't be sure,' James pointed out, feeling drained by worry. 'That's the trouble – we don't know anything for certain.'

'What now?' Mia looked to James for an answer but it was Fleur who spoke up.

'So we have to finish building our new raft as fast as we can. We have to go out there and find him.' Fleur insisted on the logic of this as she took a swig of water then handed the bottle to Mia. 'We've got plenty of rope stashed away but we need to find more canisters and some wood for oars.'

'Slow down.' Her dad frowned deeply. 'We need to think this through.'

'Dad!' she protested, her hazel eyes flashing. 'What's to think about?'

'This raft has to be strong. We can't risk going out on something that isn't seaworthy – that way we all end up in the same mess as Alfie. Your mum will agree with me when she gets back.'

'Don't you get it? Alfie's lost and he needs help!' Why couldn't he see how urgent this was? Well, if he wouldn't listen, Fleur would go ahead without him.

'Come on, Mia.'

Mia struggled to keep up as Fleur set off at a run. 'Where to?'

'To the place where Alfie found the first lot of canisters.' Fleur was already climbing the headland to the north. 'He said there was a big mess of stuff washed up in the mouth of a cave. Come on – hurry up!'

James sighed as he watched them vanish into the neighbouring bay. Yes, the girls might find what they were looking for, but even if they did, the new raft wouldn't be finished before nightfall. They would have to wait until tomorrow before they could set off. Meanwhile, Alfie was out there somewhere on the ocean, drifting helplessly on the raft or wrecked on rocks, facing a long, dark night all on his own.

Chapter Twelve

At last the sun began to sink in the west and the shadows on Alfie's small atoll lengthened. He came out of his cramped shelter, yawned, stretched then crossed the beach and waded ankle-deep into the warm water.

Pearl swam up to him, her smiling mouth open. She came almost within touching distance then backed off to tempt him deeper.

He took three or four steps down the steeply sloping sandbank until the water reached his chest then he stiffened and quickly retreated. No way would he venture out of his depth after what he'd just been through. He stepped back on to the beach, frowned and sighed.

Pearl rolled on to her side, showing him her smooth pink belly. *Take your time,* she seemed to say. *There's no hurry.*

But Alfie had felt fear rise up from the soles of his feet through his whole body. He trembled as he took refuge on the reef and it was a while before he felt calm enough to retrace his steps along its length, looking for more things that would help him survive – a coconut floating in a shallow pool would do for a start. It must have been washed ashore from a bigger island and Alfie seized it with delight. He shook it to hear the liquid inside then he took his knife from his waistband and stabbed two holes in the end. He held one hole to his mouth and drank the sweet milk, draining it to its last drop.

Saving the flesh for later, he stored the coconut under his rickety plastic roof then searched on, scouring the reef and picking up shards of polystyrene foam that he could use as a pillow when he tried to sleep. Stacking them next to the coconut, he began work on the Spiderman ball, slicing into it with the tip of his knife then sawing until he had two separate halves, each forming a bowl that would catch water next time it rained. He set them in niches on top of the reef and weighted them down by placing a rock in the bottom of each. He did the same with the empty can. Finally, as the sky turned fiery red in the west, he cracked open the shell of his precious coconut and greedily ate a portion of the white flesh – the first food he'd tasted for twenty-four hours.

As he was doing these jobs, Alfie would look up and see Pearl wallowing in the shallows of the lagoon, watching him and waiting. 'Hi,' he would say out loud. Sometimes he would stand up and wave.

Pearl chirped back at him and smacked her tail on the water. She swam in wide circles, scooping small fish into her mouth then clamping them between her rows of sharp teeth before swallowing them. *I'm not going anywhere,* her actions told him. *I'm here whenever you need me.*

*

'We only found one.' Mia's voice was flat as she showed her mum the white sunflower oil container that she and Fleur had dug out of the tangle of seaweed, old fishing nets, plastic and rope piled up outside a cave in the bay to the north. Her face was a picture of disappointment.

'We'll have to work out how to make the new raft float without canisters.' Fleur wasn't ready to give up, even though the sun was by now low in the sky at the end of Day 15 on Dolphin Island, one of the most eventful so far. 'Come on, Mia – let's go to Turtle Beach and see how far Dad has got with the platform.'

'Not now,' Katie said in a quiet, firm voice. 'It'll soon be dark.'

'But we can't stop.' Fleur knew every minute was precious if they wanted to find Alfie and bring him safely back.

'We have to,' Katie said. 'As a matter of fact, your dad got back a while ago. He took his antibiotic then I made him go inside and rest.'

Even as she spoke, the red sun slid from sight and light drained from the sky. Faint stars began to glimmer. A pale moon sailed into view.

Mia let the canister drop on to the beach with a soft thud. She cried quietly as Katie took her hand and led her inside.

'Don't get upset, honey. Let's find Monkey,' her mum whispered gently.

Fleur stayed outside, wiping tears of frustration from her cheeks. In spite of what she'd said, she knew deep down that one canister wasn't enough to keep the platform afloat and that the bamboo raft would be no good without buoyancy aids. The freshly cut canes would soon grow waterlogged and the whole thing would sink.

What can we do? she asked herself, wandering down to the water's edge. It was almost dark – the pale disc of the moon floated low in the velvety sky. Out

there somewhere, Alfie was looking at the same moon and starting to shiver with cold. Where would he spend the night? What would he eat? How would he survive?

Fleur stood a long time looking up at the sky, while out in the bay Jazz and Stormy swam in dark waters, waiting for morning to arrive.

*

Day 16. The first thing that Alfie did when he woke next morning was to mark the day. He used small shells from the beach, laying them out in a neat row

along a ledge near his shelter.

Sixteen days since the shipwreck, when his old life had been lost. This old life had meant flying from England to Australia at the start of the summer holidays then setting off on his grandfather's boat. It had been an exciting, exhilarating time of sailing the ocean all day long then going to bed in his small cabin under *Merlin*'s cockpit, of waking up and taking a shower and beginning the adventure all over again. On board they'd had everything they needed – navigation equipment, compasses, a 3G radar connected to a network system with a cockpit speaker – everything that techie-geek Alfie loved!

With a sigh he arranged the last shell in the row then checked the lagoon. Pearl was still there, thank heavens, but there was a bank of grey clouds on the horizon that made him feel uneasy and when he glanced towards the spot where he'd dragged the raft ashore, he got an unpleasant surprise. There was nothing there – no platform, no canisters – nothing!

That's weird, he thought – *I'm sure that's where I left it.* He jumped down from the rocks and sprinted along the beach looking for scuff marks in the sand, showing where he'd left the raft the day before. But the sand was smooth and damp – evidence that there'd been a high tide overnight and that the water had swept the beach clean.

High tide! The still water of the lagoon had lulled Alfie into a false sense of security. He'd forgotten about the ebb and flow of the ocean. But now that he thought about it, he realized that waves must have come in while he'd slept. They'd lapped at the abandoned raft, lifting it free of the beach and carrying it out of sight.

Seized with fresh panic, Alfie scaled the rocks to gain a better vantage point. Perhaps the tide hadn't carried the raft far. Maybe it had washed up again on the outer rim of the atoll. But no – with a clear view from the top of the reef, there was no sign of the vanished raft.

Alfie stood on the ridge and felt the wind strengthen. It chopped up the smooth surface of the water, creating small waves that broke far out to sea. A dark cormorant – black with a greenish sheen and with a hooked neck – soared on a wind current then plunged suddenly into the water, reappearing with a fish in its slender bill. On the shore three speckled sandpipers strutted and pecked in the seaweed for small shellfish.

The raft had gone for good, Alfie realized. Yesterday he'd hated every helpless second of being swept away by the wind and dragged along by currents. But that raft had been his last link with life on Dolphin Island and losing it sent a cold chill through his body.

And now clouds were rolling in towards the atoll. They soon hid the rising sun, bringing a cold, thick mist into the lagoon. Alfie needed to get back to his shelter, he realized. If rain came, at least it would provide precious water for him to drink, so he scrambled down from the low ridge then hurried along the beach, stooping to pick up another coconut and reaching his base just as the first cold splashes of rain hit his face and arms. Tilting his head back, he put out his parched tongue and caught the drops. He checked the can and the upturned halves of the Spiderman ball to make sure they were in position then he retreated into his den.

As usual, the storm was sudden and brief. A sheet of

grey mist swept in and then rain lashed Alfie's atoll. It splashed on to the flimsy plastic roof and bounced off again, dripped over the edge and ran in rivulets down on to the sand. From time to time he cupped his hands and reached out, collecting enough water to quench his thirst. He ate more coconut and sat it out until the rain passed.

*

Jazz and Stormy waited for Fleur and Mia as the sun rose on Day 16 of the Fisher family's stay on Dolphin Island. They came close to the shore and gave their signature whistles – Jazz with his high-low call and Stormy with a single shrill note that roused first Mia and then Fleur.

'Did you hear that?' Mia whispered in the grey half-light.

Immediately Fleur was alert. She nodded at Mia and gestured for her to follow her out of the shelter. They ran down the deserted beach to the water's edge. Soft white foam curled around their ankles as they waited for their dolphins to swim near.

Stormy was in the lead. He headed straight for Mia,

opening his mouth to click a message then turning and swimming a short way out to sea. He did this three times – approaching then turning with a flick of his tail, clicking all the while.

'He wants me to go with him,' Mia whispered to Fleur.

'So does Jazz.' Fleur realized that the early morning message from the dolphins was important. Jazz had raised himself out of the water and performed his tail-walking trick to entice her to follow. Now he was breaching the water with undulating movements of his body, swimming in circles and thrashing his tail.

As Mia and Fleur waded deeper, Stormy and Jazz's clicks grew louder. They swam towards the girls then nudged them with the upward-curving tips of their bottom jaws.

Fleur waited for the rush of foaming water to reach her chest before she took hold of Jazz's flipper, using it to steady herself as she slid astride his back. She made sure that Mia did the same. 'Ready?'

Sitting on Stormy and holding tight to his fin, Mia nodded. It was growing daylight but the sea was still a steely grey colour and the sky was cloudy. 'Where are we going?'

'Wherever Jazz and Stormy take us,' Fleur replied. She trusted them one hundred per cent.

'Why?' Mia's eyes widened with excitement.

Fleur felt Jazz set off towards the southern tip of the island, hugging the coast as he went and rounding the first headland into Turtle Beach ahead of Stormy and Mia. She answered Mia by raising her voice above the sound of waves breaking on the shore. 'I think the dolphins know where Alfie is!' Her head felt light as they surged through the water and her heart beat fast.

'Is that where they're taking us?' Mia asked as Stormy drew alongside Jazz. The dolphins were strong and sure. They sped through the deep green ocean.

Looking straight ahead, Fleur nodded. 'They know where he is and they want to make sure we find him. Hang on tight – here we go!'

Chapter Thirteen

Jazz and Stormy carried Fleur and Mia beyond Turtle Beach down the coast on the mile-long journey to the tip of Dolphin Island.

They swam without stopping past the mangrove swamp. Fleur and Mia held on as they swerved between rocky outcrops and rode the powerful swell until the wind grew stronger and waves loomed over them.

'More rain is on the way,' Fleur predicted through gritted teeth.

'I don't like it – I'm scared,' Mia cried as the mighty waves broke on nearby rocks. The water swirled around her and sucked at her while Stormy bravely battled the current.

'Here it comes.' Fleur felt the first drops of rain. Within seconds she was surrounded by a thick, cold mist that blocked out the coastline and made it hard to see the shapes of Mia and Stormy who followed close behind. A high wave broke over her, thrusting her sideways and almost knocking her from Jazz's back. 'Hold on, Mia,' she yelled. 'Don't let go!'

'Help!' Mia's voice sounded faint. 'I can't see you!' The rain lashed down, needle-sharp.

It was too much for the girls to cope with, the dolphins realized – the weather was too bad for them to carry on. Stormy was the first to turn and take his terrified passenger back the way they had come. Jazz went with him, battling through the storm with Fleur on his back until they reached the safety of the shallow water of their own bay.

Exhausted and struggling for breath, Mia toppled from Stormy's back and crawled on to the beach. Fleur soon joined her. Mist blinded them and dulled all sounds so that they didn't see or hear James until the last second.

He appeared out of the white fog like a shadowy ghost, calling their names at the top of his voice. 'Fleur! Mia!'

'Over here,' Fleur shouted, one arm around her sister as they emerged from the water.

He ran and picked Mia up then staggered up the beach with her. Shivering, Fleur followed them to a fire that smoked and hissed in the rain where they found Katie anxiously waiting.

'S-s-sorry,' Fleur stammered through chattering teeth and numb lips before her mum had a chance to speak. 'We went swimming with Stormy and Jazz.'

Katie let out a loud sigh of relief. 'Come inside and get dry. Didn't you notice the clouds?'

'We did but we didn't think it would be this bad.' Somehow she didn't want to give a full account of where the dolphins had carried them and why.

'We went ...' Mia began.

'... Swimming!' Fleur cut her off with a warning look. 'We thought it would just be a light shower.'

'There's no such thing as a light shower in the tropics,' James reminded them. He handed a dry T-shirt to each of the girls. 'Sunshine or storm – those are your only options in these parts.'

'Anyway, Jazz and Stormy made sure we were safe.'

Outside the rain had already started to ease and the fire revived. Fleur watched small spurts of yellow flame spring up from its crimson heart.

'No harm done, I suppose.' Waking to find Fleur and Mia missing had been a bad shock for Katie but now the relief of their safe return took over. 'What do we all want for breakfast before we start work on the raft? We have eggs or fish.'

'Eggs,' Mia said. She'd been bursting to tell James and Katie more about their adventure but Fleur had given a look that she couldn't ignore. 'Why couldn't I tell?' she hissed as their mum and dad went outside to make breakfast and she and Fleur got changed into fresh clothes.

'Because …' Fleur said with a frown. Because she was sure that her mum especially would have come down hard on them and told them not to try it again. It was too dangerous to go off by themselves. They had to wait until the raft was finished – the usual warnings.

And yet a belief had formed clear as a crystal in Fleur's mind that the dolphins were her lost brother's only hope.

Honestly, Alfie – we're coming! she vowed silently as she stood in the doorway and watched the mist clear to reveal calm water and an early morning sun. *We'll find you soon, I promise!*

*

Rainwater tasted good and the warmth of the sun felt even better. Alfie stood on his beach and drank from his handmade bowl, relishing the cool sensation on his tongue. He swished the water around his mouth then swallowed it slowly.

Refreshed, he put the bowl down carefully then waded into the water where as usual Pearl swam close to the shore.

She flicked her tail then blew out noisily through the blowhole on top of her head. Then she circled behind him and started to nudge him away from the beach down the steep slope.

Alfie went in a little way then resisted. 'I don't like it,' he tried to explain.

Pearl backed off and swam to face him. She looked at him and clicked in her usual smiley way.

'The sea – I hate it.'

Pearl came up to him and let him stroke her. *Take your time, no hurry*, was the message.

'It scares me,' he admitted as he ran his hand along the length of Pearl's soft flank, able to confess to her what he couldn't share with anyone else. 'After *Merlin* sank I had bad nightmares and then when I set sail on the raft yesterday the nightmares almost came true.' The memory made his hand tremble so he stopped stroking and took a few steps backwards.

Pearl clicked then blew out again through her nostril. It was like a deep, gentle sigh or a breath of soft wind.

'It sounds stupid,' Alfie admitted. 'I mean – I did learn to swim before we set off on this trip ...'

Pearl tilted on to one side, rocked upright then sculled slowly and easily to stay in one place. Her wide, dark eyes followed Alfie's every movement.

'The sea's so ... deep.' Unable to shrug off the memory of the irresistible pull of the current down into the murky depths, he shuddered.

Pearl made her next move. She swam away from Alfie through the clear, sparkling water to the narrow neck of the lagoon and then back again. Then she whistled quietly and waited.

Realizing that she still wanted him to swim with her, Alfie shook his head. 'I can't,' he murmured. 'I really am too scared.'

This time his dolphin seemed to understand. She stayed close while he gazed out towards the open sea, her gentle eyes looking back at him, biding her time.

*

Only the dolphins could save Alfie. As the rest of the family went off after breakfast to carry on building the raft, Fleur stayed behind.

'I'll go back and look for canisters,' she told them.

Her eye had a determined glint that reminded James of Katie. 'Yes, good idea,' he agreed.

'Good luck,' Katie told her as she, James and Mia set off for Turtle Beach.

Fleur waited until she saw them disappear over the headland then she looked out to sea and saw her special dolphin waiting by the rocks where *Merlin* had sunk. 'Hey, Jazz – this time it's down to you and me,' she murmured as she walked to the shore.

He swam towards her without any of his show-off tricks – no lob-tailing or breaching, no twists or backward flips in midair. Instead he approached calmly and held steady in the water while Fleur slid one leg over his back and grasped his dorsal fin.

'We have to sneak off,' she whispered, leaning forward to stroke him with her free hand. 'We can't let the others see us because they'll call us back and tell us not to go.'

Jazz swished his tail and set off quickly and quietly, surging through the water towards the rocks.

As they rounded the headland, Fleur caught sight of her dad and mum striding up Turtle Beach ahead of Mia towards the stand of bamboo and the half-built raft. They all had their backs to the sea. So far, so good, she thought. But there was a chance that one of them might turn around and spot her and Jazz, so she made a split-second decision to take a deep breath then slide from his back and plunge deep into the water out of sight.

In an instant Jazz followed. He was by her side, offering his flipper. She took hold of it and he picked up speed, cruising underwater until Fleur was forced to let go. She bobbed to the surface to gasp and breathe in more air. A glance at the beach told her that Mia was still lagging behind but that Katie and James had reached the bamboos and were calling for her to hurry up. Quick as a flash and hoping that she hadn't been spotted, Fleur dived again, caught hold of Jazz and they carried on beneath the waves, not surfacing again until they were clear of Turtle Beach.

'Cool – we're safe!' she gasped. Her lungs had hurt so much that she thought they would burst but they'd made it without being seen.

Alert as ever, Jazz waited for her to recover from their underwater swim. Then he invited her to climb on to his back again, easily taking her weight and heading on down the length of the island until they reached the southern tip.

'It's OK, Alfie – we're on our way.' Fleur tilted her head back and spoke the words out loud. It gave her confidence to voice her promise, making it seem more real. But, as she looked ahead at the string of coral reefs stretching from here to the neighbouring, misty island, her heart skipped a beat. There were hundreds of hidden places out there and there was no knowing where Alfie might be.

'Jazz will find you.' She raised her voice above the waves, fighting off her fear and putting all her trust in her dolphin friend.

Chapter Fourteen

The sun reached its height in a cloudless sky and Alfie took cover. Midday, Tuesday, Day 16 – so hot that all he could do was to keep to the one scrap of shade that his shelter provided. He crouched there, counting seconds, making them add up to minutes that stretched endlessly ahead. He forced himself to concentrate on numbers. Sixty seconds in one minute, sixty minutes in an hour and at least three hours before the sun lost its fierce heat and it was safe to emerge. That made ten thousand, eight hundred seconds that he had to sit out.

One, two, three, four – starting a marathon count, he drank the last of his water, chewed coconut, stared out at the nightmare, glittering sea.

People said it was beautiful down there below the

surface. They went snorkelling and scuba diving to explore the pink coral alive with fish of all colours from deepest turquoise through gold and orange to red, white and black. Divers came face to face with stingrays and squid, sponges and sea grass, they swam in and out of sunken ships that rotted and rusted on the sea bed.

But Alfie didn't see its beauty. He saw only danger.

Counting, counting, he reached three thousand, two hundred and seven. The sun still scorched the rocks but now there was a new presence in the lagoon – another young dolphin had swum into the sheltered bay to join Pearl. Alfie's face broke into a smile as he watched them play. He forgot to count the seconds.

That looks like Stormy, he thought. Mia's dolphin's back was darker grey than Pearl's and his belly was white. Hearing his long, shrill whistle, Alfie felt glad to see him.

Now where was he with counting the seconds? He'd lost track, but never mind – the sun was definitely lower in the sky. Maybe it would be OK to go into the water and cool down.

Warily Alfie crawled out from under his plastic roof and ran gingerly over the sand. He hopped quickly from one foot to the other – *ouch, ouch, hot!* Reaching the cool water, he dropped flat on his belly with a sigh of relief. *Better!*

Pearl and Stormy swam close to where he lay. Their friendly clicks drew a smile from him and enticed him deeper without him even noticing.

'Hey!' His greeting was relaxed and he reached out to put an arm over the dome of Pearl's head.

Stormy blew air through his nostril and came up on Alfie's other side. *What about me?*

'OK, OK!' Laughing, Alfie stretched his other arm around Stormy. Before he knew it they'd lifted him and carried him a little further out, setting him down where his feet could still touch the bottom.

Then Stormy swam underwater and played at making bubble rings. He came up again, his snout draped with seaweed, making it look as if he had a droopy moustache.

'Your friend is crazy,' Alfie chuckled at Pearl, who offered her fin. He took it and felt himself lifted and wafted slowly out across the lagoon. 'Whoa!' he called when he saw the ocean open up ahead of them.

Pearl heard him and changed course. She took him to the tip of the atoll and waited for him to feel the sand beneath his feet before he let go. He stood waist-deep, smiling again as Stormy joined them, still wearing his joke moustache and slapping his tail flukes on the surface to give everyone a nice cold shower.

From his new position at the exit to the lagoon, Alfie watched his dolphin friends at fresh play. He saw them breach the water in unison – once, twice, three times, out into the ocean and then back again. They soared high into the air – sleek and shiny, smiling at him with mouths wide open – coming back and beaching themselves on the gently sloping rocks to give Alfie a chance to stroke them before sliding slowly back into the green water. *Try it!* Their clicks and whistles invited him to join in.

So he copied them. He lay belly-down on the rocks and felt the waves lap against his body. He eased deeper into the water until he felt himself drift clear. *I'm floating*, he thought. *And I'm not scared. Wow!*

To either side Pearl and Stormy stayed close, like bodyguards protecting him from danger. Alfie kicked his legs and pushed with his arms. Soon he was moving away from the atoll. The dolphins remained within reach, watching his first shaky strokes through the water, free of the land.

*

Hitching a new lift with Jazz, Fleur set off from the tip of Dolphin Island, heading towards the nearest atoll. When they reached it, they circled around the dark reef at a safe distance from the rocks, making sure that this was not a place where Alfie could have landed. The rocks were too steep, the peaks too jagged, and the waves broke with too much force for anyone to set foot there.

'No chance,' Fleur said with a sigh. She sat safely astride Jazz's broad back and kept a firm hold of his fin. 'We'd better keep looking.'

So he swam on from reef to reef while Fleur kept a sharp lookout for Alfie's raft. After the third atoll she saw a flat, dark object drifting towards them. It was a few hundred metres away and her heart lurched.

If this was the remains of the bamboo raft, where was Alfie?

Jazz stopped forging ahead and waited for the mysterious object to bob closer until at last Fleur could make out the details. It was made of wood, not bamboo – an old door with a broken panel and a rusty handle that had drifted who knew how many hundreds of miles from its original home.

'OK, cool,' Fleur murmured.

At the sound of her relieved voice, Jazz swam on. He circled another, larger atoll where the rocks were smoother and more accessible. There was a cove with a beach and two palm trees, making Fleur think that if Alfie had landed here, at least he had shade and a plentiful supply of coconuts. Jazz swam in close to give her a good, clear look, but there were no footprints in the sand and no sign of either Alfie or the raft.

Fleur's raised hopes sank again and, shielding her eyes with her hand, she glanced up wearily at the sun. It was almost midday, the sky was cloudless and there was no breath of wind. Stretching ahead was a chain of atolls that were too small to land on and beyond that a couple of larger ones that seemed to encircle shallow lagoons.

'That looks more hopeful – let's head there.' She pointed due south at the nearest, biggest reef, roughly half a mile away.

Jazz heard and quickly picked up speed. He carried Fleur with ease and so fast that she had to hold on extra tight. She felt a breeze blow through her hair and a foaming bow-wave sent up a cool spray. Soon they would reach the atoll and enter the lagoon. Hopefully they would find Alfie there – and if not here then at the next one or the one after that. Fleur and Jazz would go on until they found him. They would not give in.

*

Alfie swam out of the lagoon into the open sea with Pearl and Stormy to either side. For the first time since *Merlin* was wrecked, he did not feel afraid.

Keeping his head clear of the surface, he kicked hard with his legs and moved his arms in a strong breaststroke, buoyed up by the salt water. With the dolphins close by, his confidence grew. After a while he paused and trod water, sculling with his hands and taking time to work out which direction they needed to take. He pinpointed Misty Island and took in the chain of small atolls between him and it. He needed to change direction and point north, he decided. Sure enough – there in the distance was Dolphin Island with its pyramid mountain topped by green jungle, towering over white beaches. There was the plume of grey smoke from their campfire spiralling upwards into the blue sky.

It was such a long way away – much too far for him to swim. For a moment, Alfie panicked.

Pearl sensed his fear and offered him her flipper. Stormy came up on his other side. Alfie took a firm hold.

'OK, I get it,' he breathed, looking deep into Pearl's dark eyes. 'I don't have to swim the whole way. You two are going to take me there.'

Sure enough, the dolphins set off for home. Strong and certain, they surged through the sparkling sea with Alfie safe between them, not too fast in case he grew scared or lost his grip, steadily heading north.

Alfie felt their power and he knew that as long as he

managed to hold on, he would reach home safely. With his eyes half closed to keep the spray out of his eyes, he pictured the scene of his return with the dolphins, of his worried mum and dad standing on the beach with Mia and Fleur …

'Alfie!' Astride Jazz's back, Fleur cried out in amazement. She saw him before he saw her. At first she'd only spotted two dolphins swimming in their direction, then through the spray she managed to make out a head with blond hair floating between them, hands grasping their dorsal fins. 'Alfie!' she called again.

It couldn't be real, he thought. Twice he'd imagined the sound of Fleur's voice calling him. How could that be? They were in the middle of the ocean. He felt dizzy and thought the heat must have got to him again. Then he heard her call a third time.

'It's me!' she yelled, waving wildly as Jazz set a straight course towards Alfie.

Pearl and Stormy responded with excited clicks. Pearl gave her joyful, birdlike chirp.

'Hold on!' Fleur cried as she and Jazz drew near.

Her heart filled with joy. Alfie was still alive – it was really him.

They met in the middle of the deep blue sea. Halfway between laughing and crying, Fleur slipped from Jazz's back. Pearl and Stormy made room for her to take hold of Alfie and give him a watery hug. As she held him tight, the dolphins circled and gave a volley of excited whistles.

'Listen – they're celebrating.' Fleur laughed loudly and hugged Alfie until she squeezed the breath out of him and he began to flounder.

'Whoa! Let go,' he spluttered. He flailed his arms and Pearl had to move back in to buoy him up.

'Alfie, we found you!' Fleur kept shaking her head in disbelief. 'Tell me it's not a dream – it really is you.'

'It's me,' he confirmed as he accepted a leg up from Fleur on to Pearl's back. He steadied himself then looked across at his crazy, brilliant, brave sister, who clambered astride Jazz again. 'How did you do it?'

'I didn't – Jazz did,' she explained. 'I reckon he used echolocation to keep track of Pearl and Stormy. They must have sent each other underwater signals.'

'Pearl took care of me right from the start,' Alfie confessed. 'She picked up that I was scared of the water and helped me through it. How cool is that!'

'Totally.' And wonderful and special beyond words. Fleur reached out to stroke the top of Pearl's head.

'You know you spoiled my surprise.' Alfie changed his tone from amazement to grumbling. He pretended to glower at Fleur.

'How come?'

'I was meant to arrive back on Dolphin Island all by myself. You were all supposed to be waiting there, mega worried.'

'We were,' she insisted. 'We were going nuts wondering where you were. That's why I set off with Jazz to find you.'

'Thanks – and sorry,' Alfie said stiffly when he realized the risk Fleur had taken. He could find a way to describe how grateful he felt without all his feelings spilling out in a big mess.

'OK, cool,' she muttered. *Is that it?* she thought. *Is that all I get for trying to save your life?*

'I mean it.' He glanced across at her then, switching

the subject, added sheepishly, 'I lost the raft. Do you think Mum and Dad will be mad?'

'Yep,' she predicted. 'But not so much about the raft. They'll be mad with you because you broke the rules.'

He sighed and nodded. 'The not-going-anywhere-by-yourself rule?'

'Yep,' she said again. This was going to be a tough home-coming.

'What about you? You broke the rule just like me.'

'True.' Fleur couldn't deny it.

'Dude, are we in trouble,' he sighed.

'Better get it over with, huh?'

Alfie frowned then took a deep breath. 'OK, I'm ready. Let's go.'

With Stormy swimming ahead, Pearl and Jazz set off for home with their precious cargo. Soon Fleur and Alfie could see the tip of the island and beyond that the familiar sights of the mangrove swamp and the inlets along the rocky coastline. They held on tight and kept their fingers crossed as the dolphins passed Turtle Beach and finally rounded the last headland into their bay.

Chapter Fifteen

It was nearing the end of the afternoon and Mia sat on the rocks holding Monkey, feeling miserable. Day 16 had been a very bad day – the worst since their boat had been wrecked in the storm and they'd been cast ashore on Dolphin Island.

'First Alfie vanishes, now Fleur,' Katie had said when she, James and Mia had returned from Turtle Beach and realized that Fleur was nowhere to be seen. She and James had tried not to let Mia see how upset they were, but Mia could tell.

'Don't worry, Mi-mi – Alfie and Fleur will be back soon,' James had told her with a quavering voice as Katie had climbed the cliff to the lookout. 'Mum's gone to see if she can spot them from up there. Before you know it, we'll be sitting round the fire listening to their adventures.'

Mia had longed to believe him but she'd still felt scared. 'The bad thing is – right now nobody knows where they are,' she'd whispered to Monkey as she carried him down to the sea. All she could do was stay on the rocks and wait, she decided.

So now she sat, trying not to cry and wishing they would return. *Who's going to help me collect feathers if Alfie doesn't come home soon?* she wondered. *And how can I make shell necklaces without Fleur?*

She waited the rest of the afternoon, listening to waves break on the shore. She didn't know how long she sat looking out to sea, only that the sun was sinking and long shadows stretched across the beach but there was still no sign of either Alfie or Fleur.

'They're not coming home,' she mumbled to Monkey who rested limply in the crook of her arm.

Mia stood up and took one last look. A lone dolphin swam into the bay. He cut cleanly through the calm water, heading straight towards her. 'Stormy!' she yelled.

He came right up to the beach and gave his high whistle. He swam out a little way then rolled to show her his white belly. Overjoyed, she dropped Monkey on a rock and ran into the water to join him.

Then, before she had time to take it all in, two more dolphins swam into the sparkling bay. They carried passengers – one dressed in a striped T-shirt and blue shorts, the other in a white T-shirt and denim shorts.

'Oh, wow!' Mia stood transfixed.

Fleur and Alfie knew they were almost home. They saw Stormy swimming in the shallows and Mia standing still as a statue close to the shore – a tiny figure in a crazy sunhat with red and yellow feathers sticking up from its brim.

'Dad, come quick!' Mia turned towards the shelter, her voice high and strained. She swung round to study the approaching dolphins. Yes, she was sure it was them – Pearl and Jazz carrying Alfie and Fleur safely home.

Mia took off her hat then flung herself forward and started to swim towards them. Suddenly she felt Stormy come up behind her and push against her feet, propelling her forward at high speed.

'Here comes turbocharged Supergirl!' Fleur said with a laugh. She leaned sideways and slipped from

Jazz's back, ready to greet her little sister.

Alfie too slid into the sea. He let Mia squeal and hug him then drag him towards the shore. Together Fleur, Mia and Alfie staggered on to the beach.

Up by the campfire, James looked to see what all the fuss was about. He was joined by Katie, fresh from her latest trek up to the lookout.

'Look at that. Can you believe it!' he gasped as she overtook him and sprinted to the water. Forgetting about the pain, he ran to keep up.

Dripping and laughing, Alfie, Fleur and Mia stumbled out of the water, arms linked, to face the music.

'Wait for it,' Fleur muttered under her breath.

But, to their surprise, there was no telling-off, no talk of rules, no demand for explanations.

'It's OK. Don't say anything.' James threw his arms around Alfie and hugged him.

'Come here,' Katie whispered to Fleur. She slid her arm around her waist. 'Thank goodness you're both safe.' The tears she cried were tears of joy.

In the shallow water, Pearl, Jazz and Stormy watched the reunion. The lost boy was back safely in the arms of his family. All was as it should be.

In unison the dolphins turned and started to swim out to sea. They synchronized their actions – three grey torpedoes cutting through the smooth surface as the sun set over the headland, breaching together, arching high out of the water and in again with scarcely a splash.

'Bye, Stormy!' Mia called after them.

Alfie, Fleur, James and Katie were just in time to look up and see the dolphins swim away. They raised their arms and hollered goodbye.

The three youngsters breached again. They dived down then reappeared to slap their tail flukes on the water before they swam on.

'Stay safe,' Fleur called after them.

'And thank you, Pearl,' Alfie said with a long sigh.

Soon the dolphins were gone and, holding hands, the family headed up the beach.

Before nightfall they needed to fetch more wood for the fire and fresh water from the waterfall. There was fish to be cooked and fruit to be sliced, macaque monkeys to be chased away and shells and parrots' feathers collected for necklaces and hats.

'Promise me,' Fleur said to Alfie when the jobs were done and she and Mia strolled with him on the quiet beach. Their faces were clear and pale in the moonlight; their dark eyes shone. As always the ceaseless waves rolled on to the shore.

'What?' he asked, glancing up the beach at Katie and James standing arm in arm by the fire.

She looked him in the eye. 'Don't try that again, OK?'

Alfie wrinkled his nose then nodded. 'OK. No more going off by myself and getting lost. From now on we stick together.'

'Together,' Fleur echoed.

'Cool,' Mia murmured. She smiled up at them both. 'Race you!' she said as she broke into a run up the beach.

'What do you reckon?' Alfie asked Fleur.

She and Alfie were safe. They were tired. But they could never resist a challenge. 'Let's go!' she said with a grin.

So together they sprinted after Mia for all they were worth.

The story continues in ...

Turn the page for a sneak peek ...

Chapter One

'I can see a ship!' Mia cried. She pointed to the horizon. 'Ship! Ship!'

From their lookout ledge high on the rugged hill, Fleur and Alfie strained to see.

'Where?' Fleur demanded. The blue sea sparkled; the sinking sun gradually turned the sky pink.

'There!' Mia jumped up and down as she waved and pointed. 'Help!' she yelled at the distant container ship. 'We're stuck on Dolphin Island. Come and rescue us … please!'

'They won't hear you,' Fleur muttered. Ah yes, she saw it – a faraway ship, so small she couldn't make out any details. It was the first they'd spotted for days. 'Hurry – let's put more wood on the fire. Maybe they'll see the smoke.'

Alfie lugged two heavy branches along the ledge and flung them on the fire. Sparks flew and flames licked at the wood. Smoke rose high into the clear sky.

'This way – look over here!' Mia cried.

The ship sailed steadily from east to west, crawling along the horizon with its heavy cargo.

'Please! …' Mia held her breath and watched it sail on without altering course. '… It's not coming,' she whimpered at last.

The sun sank further in the west and smoke billowed from their fire into their eyes.

'What's up? Why are you crying?' Alfie flung the gruff questions at Fleur as he threw a final log into the flames.

'I'm not. It's the smoke,' she sniffed. The sailors hadn't seen their signal. Hope of rescue faded with the dying light.

'Why didn't they see us?' Mia wanted to know. Her dirty cheeks were streaked with what were definitely tears.

'It was too far away,' Fleur explained. She tried to cover her disappointment for Mia's sake. 'Don't worry

– someone will come looking for us before too long. We won't have to stay here for ever.'

'It only feels like forever,' Alfie grumbled.

It was Day 17 on Dolphin Island – two and a half long weeks since the storm had driven their boat *Merlin* on to the rocks and cast the family into the sea. They'd all made it to the shore – Alfie, plus his younger sister, Mia, then Fleur, the oldest of the three kids, and their mum and dad. Their dad, James, was injured but everyone was safe. They'd built a camp and two fires, found fresh water, foraged and fished and found a way to survive.

'Hang on a second.' Mia rubbed the tears from her eyes and began to point once more. 'I can see something.'

Alfie and Fleur sighed and shook their heads.

'No, look!' There was movement far out to sea. Half a dozen curved fins cut rapidly through the water. A sleek grey shape leaped clear of the waves, then another and another. Others joined them and the creatures arced through the air then disappeared with a splash of their mighty tails.

'Oh, wow – cool!' Alfie breathed.

Dolphins! Not just any dolphins, but their special pod – all swimming swiftly in the white wake of the gigantic ship, rushing to catch up and attract the attention of the men on board.

'Go, Jazz! Go, Stormy! Go, Pearl!' Fleur yelled.

The three kids held their breaths again and watched as the dolphins sped alongside the ship, tiny from this distance and impossible to make out who was who. They breached the water and twisted and rolled in midair, disappeared under the frothing, foaming waves then came up to the surface again. They surged ahead and circled around the bow-wave made by the enormous vessel as it cut through the clear turquoise water.

'Oh – don't get too close!' Fleur was worried for Jazz and the others. The ship was as big as a block of flats, casting an enormous shadow, powering on.

'I think they're trying to steer the ship around, to make them notice our fire.' Alfie was the one who figured it out. He'd read in a book about marine mammals that dolphins were smart and brave enough to help in this way. 'More branches!' he muttered as he fed the flames on their ledge at Lookout Point.

'Too close!' Fleur groaned. She put a hand over her eyes, unable to look.

The dolphins swam in formation ahead of the ship, by now an indistinct black block silhouetted against a crimson sun. They did everything they could to make it turn around.

More adventures on Dolphin Island

Six books to collect!